# THE HOME BOOK OF TURKISH COOKERY

# THE HOME BOOK OF
# *Turkish Cookery*

**VENICE LAMB**
*With line drawings by the author*

FABER AND FABER
LONDON & BOSTON

*First published in 1969*
*First published in this edition 1973*
*Reprinted 1975 and 1978*
*by Faber and Faber Limited*
*3 Queen Square London WC1*
*Printed in Great Britain by*
*Whitstable Litho Ltd., Whitstable*


*ISBN 0 571 10390 1*

## ACKNOWLEDGEMENTS

I would like to thank most warmly all the people who helped me to collect recipes in Turkey and who gave me so much of their time and put up so patiently with my questions; especially Mr. and Mrs. Ruhi Akinci, Mrs. Nitral Atatur, Mrs. Servet Korkmaz, Mrs. Sabiha Elmer, Mrs. Sermin Erol, Miss Aysegul Dora and Mr. Sukiu Babuzoglu. I would also like to thank Miss Susan Foulston of the British Information Service in Istanbul and Mr. Philip Jannetta of the British Council in Ankara, who gave me much help and encouragement. Lastly I would like to thank my husband for his generosity in enabling me to travel in Turkey over the years and for his help and interest during the preparation of this manuscript.

# CONTENTS

# *Introduction*

Turkey, situated as she is between Europe and Asia, forms a culinary buffer zone between the hot spicy food of the Orient and the plainer cooking of the West. She is surrounded by countries which all possess widely different cooking patterns. Her most western section is still part of Europe. A close link exists between Turkey and her Balkan neighbours and as she overran so much of the Balkans in the past, there has inevitably been an exchange of cooking traditions. The long Mediterranean coast line and common borders with Syria and Iraq bring her into contact with the Arab world and the cuisines of the Middle East: her eastern borders touch on Iran and Armenia, with whom she shares tastes of a more Central Asian nature. The constant movement of various peoples into Turkey throughout her long history has enabled her to assimilate all these various cooking patterns into what now forms a distinct Turkish cuisine.

Turkish cooking has evolved from basic simple peasant food; straightforward and practical, using ingredients at hand and presenting them to their best advantage. This type of cooking can be done under any conditions, from the sophisticated modern kitchens in Istanbul with gas stoves, electric mixers and pressure cookers, to wood-burning ranges or simple open pit fires in the centre of the village home. The only difference between the peasant meal and the sultan's banquet is in the quantity of dishes and the expensive extra garnishes. A dish of stewed vegetables will be the same wherever one eats it and just as good: the Turks possess an instinct that knows how to bring out the best in any food. However humble the dish may be, it will always be well cooked and attractively served.

I have cooked a *şiş kebab* and a pilaf equally well in the middle of a field on an open wood fire as I have in my kitchen at home. I feel this bears out the point that most of Turkish cooking has evolved from generations of practical-minded nomads who cooked out in the open and who developed a type of food that could be prepared and eaten easily or re-cooked at a later time if necessary. Turkish food reflects this background as it tends to take the form of small bundles or to be rolled into balls which I presume allowed it to be easily carried around and heated up over fires out in the steppe where shepherds might find themselves while following their herds. Much of the time taken in the preparation of Turkish dishes consists in reducing the food to the small sizes which are so typical of the *köftes*, *dolmas*, *mantıs* and *böreks*. Another characteristic feature is the composite dish which combines all that one needs for a meal in a single confection, as, for example, so many of the versatile casseroles in which Turkish cooking abounds.

It is the unexpected combination of ingredients that surprises one in Turkish food; and this provides an unending source of fascination when travelling, to discover what other people do with food. Turkish cooking is full of contrasts such as poached eggs in cold yogurt, fried mussels with a walnut sauce or cold garlic vegetable stews to mention only a few. Each dish is savoured for itself and is therefore always served separately; this gives the impression of many courses but to my mind is the pleasantest way of enjoying a dish. The natural instinct that every Turk has for serving a balanced meal will guarantee a gastronomic delight.

The average Turkish housewife will expect to do a lot of hard and patient work in the preparation of her meals and will not have many modern appliances to help her. She will probably use hand-made wooden utensils such as ladles, mortars and spoons and will cook in large brass or copper pots and trays and will spend many hours stirring these over a large black wood-burning stove which requires constant stoking. Although these stoves may appear tiresome and old fashioned to many, they do in fact produce by far the most delicious results. All the meals that I have cooked on them have always turned out the best: there is something about the woody flavour that cannot be captured with gas or electricity. The Turkish cook manipulates her ingredients with a sure touch and a dexterity which has produced a wonderful array of dishes, both as varied and as fascinating as the architecture and cultures with which she is surrounded. Her skill reflects in its richness the subtle merging of peoples both from the Arab world of the eastern Mediterranean and that of the Balkans and Asia.

There is an unlimited list of sumptuous dishes to be had in Turkey and this book will only serve as an introduction to their possibilities. I hope it may act as a stimulant to any would-be traveller who may feel tempted to sample them in their original setting.

X

## GUIDE TO TURKISH DISHES IN COMMON USE

**Ayran** A yogurt drink mixed with water and salt

**Baklava** A Turkish mille-feuilles pastry

**Börek** This refers to a vast array of savoury or sweet fillings which are wrapped up in a paper-thin pastry in various shapes and sizes

**Dolma** This means stuffed food, or stuffing that is wrapped up in leaves or fillings of any kind

**Güvec** Casserole dishes cooked in earthenware pots

**Helva** A name for many kinds of sweets made with flour, honey, butter, sesame seeds or semolina etc., which are formed into squares or pressed into hard pieces

**Kadayıf** A kind of crumpet, usually soaked in syrup

**Kebab** Refers to most meat dishes and does not necessarily mean meat that is cut up into cubes. The dish is described in the word which comes before *kebab*, i.e. *şiş kebab*

**Köfte** This refers to any food that is minced up and rolled into little balls or sausages; usually meat, fish or potatoes: rissoles

**Lokma** A sweet pastry

**Lokum** Turkish Delight, a soft transparent sweet

X

## *Guide to Turkish Dishes in Common Use*

**Mantı** A kind of water pastry stuffed with meat and boiled like a ravioli

**Meze** Hors d'œuvre

**Pide** A soft white flat bread baked in rounds and used in many savoury dishes

**Pilâki** A cold stew of fish or vegetables cooked in olive oil or garlic

**Pilâv** Rice cooked with stock and flavourings

**Simit** A ring of crusty bread baked with sesame seeds

**Turşu** Pickles

**Yahni** A hot stew of meat and vegetables served in its broth

**Yufka** Sheets of paper-thin pastry

## GLOSSARY OF INGREDIENTS AND THEIR USES IN TURKISH COOKING

**Cayenne** A hot red powder made from ground chillies which should be used very sparingly.

**Celeriac** Long celery is not usually available in Turkey but *celeriac* and its leaves are used quite a lot. In dishes where celeriac would be used I have put in celery as well as it makes an excellent substitute and is more easily available in the west. Either can be used equally well.

**Chick peas** These are called *nohut* in Turkish and are very like a sort of round haricot bean. They need long soaking before use and take rather a lot of boiling to get soft.

**Cream** A thick cream called *kaymak* which is a cream made from buffalo milk is commonly used in Turkey with cakes and pastries. *Kaymak* has a strong flavour of its own. However, Devonshire cream makes a very good substitute as it has the right consistency. This can easily be made at home by scalding fresh thick cream for about two minutes when it will form clots. It also keeps well.

**Cummin** This spice looks rather like caraway seed, but it has a pungent curry flavour of its own and is frequently used in meat dishes. It should be roughly crushed in a mortar before use to release its full fragrance.

**Fennel** Fresh fennel is used a lot with fish in Turkey and has an aniseed flavour. It is also very pleasant with artichokes and other cold vegetables. It can usually be bought dry in England.

**Flour** The white flour commonly used in Turkey is a *plain* flour and a plain flour is used in all the recipes.

**Maize flour** This yellow flour is made from ground corn (maize) and has a slightly gritty texture. It is called corn flour in America and polenta in Italy. It is ground in three grades, fine, medium and coarse. When it is to be used for cakes the fine grade is best, the coarser grades are better for porridge and other dishes. It seems to be best known as 'polenta' in shops in England.

**Olive oil** Turkey produces excellent olive oil which is in constant use in the kitchen. Failing Turkish olive oil, any pure *olive* oil will do as well. Other types of cooking oil should not be used as a substitute for olive oil as they give a different taste and change the whole flavour of the dish. Olive oil is always used in dishes that are served cold as it will not congeal.

**Paprika** As the name suggests, this powder is made from ground red peppers and is much milder than cayenne powder. It is frequently used in Turkish food and a little pot is nearly always on the table with the other condiments so that a pinch can be added at will.

**Parsley** The parsley grown in Turkey is usually the Continental or 'French' parsley. This has a larger leaf and a stronger flavour than the English varieties. It can be bought from many markets in England or can easily be grown at home along with the ordinary parsley. It will be noted that parsley is in great demand in Turkish dishes, and either variety is more or less essential to the success of the dish. How much should be used in each dish is very much up to the individual and whether it is a strong or mild parsley. The amounts that I have given are intended as an approximate guide and can be adjusted according to taste. A little fresh parsley grown in the garden or in a pot is a real boon and essential to good cooking. Fresh sage, thyme and mint are also used a lot in Turkey and can also be grown easily. Although most herbs are used fresh in Turkish food, this should not deter the enthusiast from using dry herbs, working on the principle that any herbs are better than none!

**Pine nuts** Slightly elongated little white nuts rather like an enlarged grain of rice. They are used in pilafs and meat dishes or just eaten by themselves. They can be bought from the shops listed on page 24.

**Pistachio** These green nuts are the most delicious and prized of all the nuts in Turkey. They can be bought fresh or roasted and salted and are quite expensive even in Turkey. They enhance any dish with their unique flavour and are a joy to eat on their own as well.

**Rice** In all the savoury dishes employing rice, the *long grain* variety should be used. Round pudding rice should never be used for making pilafs as the result will be a sticky mess. For the preparation of rice before it is cooked, see the pilaf section.

**Saffron** This is a light yellow powder, apparently taken from the stigma of crocuses, and is used to turn pilafs a delicate yellow.

**Turmeric** This is a much stronger and darker yellow powder which is used a lot in curries and can also be used for pilafs. Not more than a teaspoon need be added to any amount of pilaf to render it a bright yellow! It has a slightly musty flavour.

**Vanilla** In recipes that call for vanilla, a much better flavour will result if *vanilla pods* are used instead of vanilla essence. The pods should be allowed to infuse in the warm milk or water to be used, for a few minutes and then they can be removed and kept for another time. The pods can be easily obtained at chemists or health food shops and they last for ages.

**Vine leaves** These are most easily gathered in countries where the grapes grow. They are usually fresh in Turkey, but can be bought in tins in Soho. Cabbage makes a very good substitute and is actually much tastier. It is also often used in Turkey. To prepare vine leaves before use see the individual recipes.

**Wheat** Wheat grains are used a lot in Turkish cooking and form a valuable staple food to supplement meat. *Bulgur* is a whole wheat that is untreated and needs to be soaked in water before use and then boiled for several hours. It is made into a kind of porridge and used to give body to other dishes. *Buğday* is whole meal ground wheat and *Yarma* is cracked wheat grains sometimes called grit. Their uses are described in the individual recipes.

# HERBS

| | | | |
|---|---|---|---|
| *Adaçayı* | Sage | *Kekik* | Thyme |
| *Biberiye* | Rosemary | *Maydanoz* | Parsley |
| *Defne Yaprağı* | Bay leaf | *Nane* | Mint |
| *Dereotu* | Dill | *Razene* | Fennel |
| *Fesleğen* | Basil | *Tarhun* | Tarragon |
| *Frenk maydanozu* | Chervil | | |

# SPICES

| | | | |
|---|---|---|---|
| *Biber* | Black pepper | *Küçük Hindistancevizi* | |
| *Cemen (kimyon)* | Cummin | | Nutmeg |
| *Hardal* | Mustard | *Sarmısak* | Garlic |
| *Kakule* | Cardamon | *Sirke* | Vinegar |
| *Karaman kimyonu* | Caraway | *Tarçın* | Cinnamon |
| *Karanfil* | Clove | *Tuz* | Salt |
| *Kırmızı biber* | Paprika | *Zencefil* | Ginger |
| *Kişniş* | Coriander | *Zerdeçav* | Turmeric |

## SOME USEFUL TURKISH NAMES

| | | | |
|---|---|---|---|
| *Bal* | Honey | *Piliç* or *tavuk* | Chicken |
| *Balık* | Fish | *Sebze* | Vegetables |
| *Çay* | Tea | *Şeker* | Sugar |
| *Ciğer* | Liver | *Şiğir* | Beef |
| *Dana* | Veal | *Su* | Water |
| *Et* | Meat | *Süt* | Milk |
| *İşkembe* | Tripe | *Tavuk* or *piliç* | Chicken |
| *Kahve* | Coffee | *Un* | Flour |
| *Kuzu* | Lamb | *Yumurta* | Eggs |
| *Meyva* | Fruit | *Zeytin* | Olive |
| *Peynir* | Cheese | *Zeytinyağı* | Olive oil |

X

## A BRIEF NOTE ON PRONUNCIATION

Turkish is a straightforward language to pronounce and generally speaking each syllable is given its full value and all are equally stressed.

**The vowels**

*a* is pronounced like the continental rather than the English a. A cross between as in 'cat' and 'cut'.

*e* as in 'pet'.

*ı*, the undotted ı which does not exist in English, is a cross between 'bit' and 'but'.

*i* as in 'bit', or when lengthened by a following ğ or y as in 'been'.

*o* as in 'jolly'.

*ö* is the same sound pronounced at the front of the mouth—as the German ö or, in English, 'earn'.

*u* as in 'bush'.

*ü*, again the same sound pronounced at the front of the mouth—as the French 'tu'.

**The consonants** are pronounced as in English except for:

*c* as in 'jam'.

*ç* as in 'chair'.

*ş* as in 'ship'.

*g* is hard as in 'goat'.

*ğ* is silent.

# LIST OF LONDON SHOPS WHICH STOCK TURKISH GROCERIES

EAST AND WEST STORES
119 Westbourne Grove, W.2. 01 229 6336

HELLENIC PROVISION STORES LTD.
25 Charlotte Street, W.1. 01 687 4406

MEDITERRANEAN FOOD STORES
13 Blenheim Crescent, Portobello Road, W.11.

OLYMPIA STORES
Delancey Street, N.W.1. 01 387 8767

# A NOTE ON THE USE OF THE RECIPES IN THIS BOOK

While preparing this book I became very conscious of the difficulty of conveying in the recipes the right balance of herbs, spices and seasoning without being either arbitrary or vague. It is almost impossible to give precise instructions in the use of herbs and seasoning, as it depends so much on individual taste and the cook's own 'feel' as she goes along, yet to be too indefinite about it can be unnerving to those who do not feel so sure or who have had very little experience. The Turkish cook will take a bit from here and a pinch from there and put it all together without stopping to measure it and to capture this in the recipes is a very hard task!

In the ingredient lists, therefore, I have tried to give a near approximation for the herbs and seasoning, which I hope the experienced cook will not treat rigidly, while it might be of some help to the beginner. I would like to stress that most Turkish dishes call for some herbs and to omit them altogether would render the dishes quite uncharacteristic. In the same way the use of garlic is important and to do without it would destroy the intrinsic flavour, whereas a little more or less will not do excessive injury. In the long run the best guide to seasoning is constant tasting and experiment.

In the use of large vegetables such as onions, potatoes, tomatoes, aubergines and marrows I have given a quantity and an approximate size, rather than a weight, which I find both more useful and quicker when cooking and is also more in keeping with the Turkish housewife who would also work this way. In most of the vegetable dishes an *exact* amount is not called for and a *near* quantity will be quite in balance with the rest of the ingredients. For example, I have put 'two large aubergines' which is easier to select than a definite weight which two aubergines might not add up to! Onions are put down as small, medium and large and I feel it can be safely left to the individual to gauge the right amount. For the preparation of unfamiliar vegetables, I have given a detailed account in the beginning of the vegetable section.

It should be remembered when serving raw onions, that a mild variety are used in Turkey which are specially grown for eating raw and these can be bought in England under the name of 'salad' onions. They are round and white and should not be confused with spring onions or small pickle onions.

Most of the recipes will feed from four to six people.

The oven temperatures are given as slow, moderate and hot, with the Fahrenheit temperature in parentheses. A comparative oven guide will be found in the beginning of the book as well as a list of weights and measures.

For some of the more unfamiliar dishes, I have provided diagrammatic sketches which I hope will make it easier to see what one is aiming at.

## OVEN TEMPERATURES

| | *Degrees Fahrenheit* | *Regulo Mark* |
|---|---|---|
| Very slow | 250 to 275 | ¼, ½ |
| Slow | 300 to 325 | 1, 2 |
| Moderate | 350 to 375 | 3, 4, 5 |
| Hot | 400 to 425 | 6, 7 |
| Very hot | 450 to 475 | 8, 9 |

## MEASUREMENTS

In the measurements in this book I have used pounds and ounces although in Turkey they use kilograms. One kilogram equals two pounds three ounces, which is an awkward amount and generally tends to be too much for average use. For cup measurements I mean a breakfast cup which holds roughly eight fluid ounces and is not quite so large as the standard U.S. measuring cup. For tablespoon I mean an ordinary household serving spoon which holds one ounce of flour.

# *Hors d'œuvre*

Turkey is a great place for little tasty snacks and morsels which accompany drinks of any kind, such as an aperitif, or a mid-morning coffee with a friend. They also arrive at the start of a meal. These delicious titbits cover a wide range of foods, both hot and cold, raw and cooked.

Some of the most common *meze*, as these are called, are black and green olives; a white salty goat cheese with a strong flavour; and a vast array of nuts, the roasted and salted *pistachio*, being perhaps the nicest. There is, as well, caviar, which is comparatively cheap coming from the Black Sea, and many sorts of salted fish, sardines and shell fish. Fried mussels and prawns are particularly good, fresh from the sea, crisp and juicy. There are various types of sausage, such as *sucuk*, and a dried spicy beef sausage called *pastırma*, which can be eaten hot or cold.

Among the hot dishes one finds the *börek* family of little meat and cheese pasties; the grilled tiny *köftes*, which are miniature-sized meat balls; and an interesting dish of grilled intestines called *kokoreç*, which is often sold in the streets and served with fresh thyme.

Many of the cold stuffed *dolmas* are served as a *meze*, especially the stuffed vine leaves. The recipes for these will be in the vegetable section. I have also included many salads which are equally good as hors d'œuvres.

Here I have given some of the more unusual *meze* which I liked. As well as being a good start to any meal, they are extremely useful to hand round at parties.

**Yalancı Dolma** COLD STUFFED VINE LEAVES

*Fresh vine leaves or cabbage leaves*
1 *tablespoon olive oil*
*Juice of* 1 *lemon*

For the stuffing:

1 *medium onion*
4 *ozs uncooked rice*
2 *ozs currants*
2 *ozs pine nuts*
1 *tablespoon chopped parsley*
*Pinch of allspice and cinnamon*
*Salt and black pepper to taste*
1 *tablespoon tomato purée*

Chop up the onion finely and fry it in the olive oil until it becomes transparent. Wash and rinse the rice well and add it to the onion and fry them both for a few minutes more, stirring well together; then add just enough water to cover the rice, and the rest of the ingredients for the stuffing except the tomato purée. Cook them all until the rice is dry. Stir in the tomato purée to moisten the rice mixture a little.

Wash the leaves and cut out the central vein; if using tinned vine leaves, rinse them carefully in cold water and spread them out on a cloth to dry. Take care not to break them as they are rather fragile after being soaked in brine. Put a teaspoon of the stuffing in the centre of each leaf and fold it up securely into a little package and pack it tightly into the bottom of a stew pot. Between each layer of *dolmas*, place some more leaves. When all are ready and wedged into the pot, press an inverted saucer on top of them and cover with water, some lemon juice and seasoning to the level of the saucer. Close the lid of the pot and simmer them for an hour and then allow them to cool as they are in the pot. Drain off the water and arrange them on a platter and chill well before serving them.

**Poca** CHEESE IN PASTRY

1 *egg*
½ *pint yogurt*
*As much flour as it takes to make a soft dough*

*2 tablespoons olive oil*
*½ lb margarine*
*½ teaspoon baking powder*
*1 teaspoon salt*
*¼ lb soft white cheese*
*A small bunch chives*
*3 or 4 sprigs parsley*

Melt the margarine and pour it into a bowl with the egg, yogurt and olive oil and beat them well together; gradually add in the flour, salt and baking powder until you have a manageable dough which should then be kneaded for about five minutes until it becomes smooth and soft. If it feels very oily, store it in the refrigerator or a cool place until it hardens a little before use. Meanwhile prepare the stuffing by mixing the cream cheese with a little seasoning and the finely chopped chives and parsley.

Now break off a little piece of the dough about the size of a small egg and roll it between your palms until you have a smooth ball. Make a hole in the side of the ball by pushing in a finger and open it up a little and force into it a teaspoonful of the cream cheese mixture and then close up the hole again. It takes a little practice to get them neat. Although the shape of the balls does not really matter, one should aim at getting them as uniform as possible so that they will look attractive when they are baked. Arrange them all on a greased baking tray, brush over with milk and bake in a hot oven (400) for twenty minutes. Serve them hot with pickles or chutney.

**Patates Köftesi** STUFFED POTATO BALLS

*6 medium potatoes*
*½ lb minced lamb or beef*
*1 large onion*
*1 large tomato or 2 small ones*
*1 oz butter*
*2 eggs*
*2 cloves garlic*
*Salt and pepper*
*Olive oil for deep frying*

Boil the potatoes in their skins and then peel them into a large bowl: mash them thoroughly with one egg and plenty of salt and pepper. Heat the butter in a frying pan and gently fry the finely sliced onion until it becomes transparent, then add the mince, skinned tomato and the crushed garlic. Season the meat and continue to fry until it becomes dry. Knead the potatoes well with your hand and then take out just enough to form little patties about the size of a small saucer. This is done by pressing the potato gently from side to side between the palms until the patty is formed. Put about one teaspoonful of the meat in the centre of the patty and fold the patty around the meat until it forms a ball. Roll the balls a little between the palms to make them secure. When all are ready, dip them into some beaten egg and fry them in deep oil until they are golden. Serve them with a hot spicy sauce or pickle.

NOTE These potato balls can be made either small or large, according to how you want them. If they are served as *meze* they should be quite small and dainty.

**Patates Köftesi** POTATO FINGERS

*4 or 5 medium potatoes*
*½ lb grated white cheese (Cheshire would be nearest to a Turkish white cheese)*
*1 oz flour*
*1 egg*
*2 or 3 sprigs parsley*
*Salt and black pepper*
*2 tablespoons olive oil for frying*

Boil the potatoes and mash them well; cool and add the cheese, egg and flour. Season well and mix in the chopped parsley. Knead thoroughly and form into fingers. Fry in very hot olive oil, drain and serve with some hot chillies or sliced peppers.

**Sardalya Tavası** FRIED SARDINES

The fresh sardines from the Sea of Marmara are a great favourite; they are cleaned and then wiped dry and tossed in seasoned flour and fried in deep oil for a few minutes and eaten piping hot with rock salt and lemon. They must be very fresh and in season for the best results.

**Sardalya Sarması** SARDINES IN VINE LEAVES

Fresh sardines are used for this dish, but sprats could be substituted equally well.

Wash and clean the sardines and cut off the head and tail. Wrap each one in a vine leaf and rub it well in olive oil. Heat the olive oil until smoking hot and fry the sardines quickly until crisp on each side. Serve very hot with lemon juice and pepper.

**Kabak Tavası** FRIED COURGETTES

| | |
|---|---|
| 4 *courgettes or baby marrows (or as many as required)* | 2 *cloves garlic* |
| 2 *tablespoons olive oil* | 2 *tablespoons vinegar* |
| | *Salt* |

Wash the courgettes and slice them and sprinkle them with salt and leave aside for about fifteen minutes; rinse and pat dry. Heat the oil and fry the crushed garlic in it for a second and then brown the courgettes on both sides, taking care not to break them. Arrange them on a serving dish and pour a little vinegar over them while they are still hot and leave for a few minutes and then drain the vinegar off and serve them hot.

**Midye Tavası** FRIED MUSSELS

Fried mussels are a common sight at the street corners, where the vendor sits frying them as people come up to him to buy them. They are threaded on little wooden skewers and sold at three per stick.

Scrub the mussels well and immerse them in water. Take one out at a time and force it open with a sharp knife and scoop out the flesh; trim off the black part and the beard (this is the fibrous bit which attaches it to the shell) and leave them in some cold water until they are needed.

Prepare a deep pan of boiling oil, a bowl of seasoned flour and another bowl of cold water. Dip each mussel into the flour, then into the water and then drop it carefully into the hot oil, avoiding the spitting. Fry them until they are golden and serve hot. The mussel is dipped into a little bowl of tarator sauce (page 134) which is placed beside each plate.

NOTE Mussels should always be bought tightly closed as this ensures that they are fresh. If they prove too difficult to open, they should be washed and then placed wet in a strong pot and steamed for a few minutes (which is done by putting the pot over a hot plate with the lid on). The mussels will soon start to open themselves. Then proceed as above.

**Beyin** BRAINS OR SWEETBREADS

This recipe is equally good with brains or sweetbreads. Wash them well under running water and then blanche them by placing them in cold water and bringing it rapidly to the boil; throw this water away and cover with fresh water, adding salt and pepper, and simmer them for about half an hour. Take the brains out of the water and cool them a little and then cut them up into small pieces the size of a walnut and into them mix a tablespoon of olive oil, the juice of a lemon, a little chopped parsley, some salt and black pepper. Serve them cold.

**Beyin Tavası** FRIED BRAINS

Blanche the brains or sweetbreads as above and then dip them into seasoned flour and fry them in hot oil until they are golden; arrange on a warm dish and squeeze lemon juice over them and sprinkle with paprika.

**Koç Yumurtası Tavası** FRIED RAMS TESTICLES

Cut the testicles into halves and dip in seasoned flour and beaten egg and fry in hot oil until they are brown. Serve with a lemon and parsley sauce (see page 134).

**Patlıcan Tavasi** FRIED AUBERGINES

Peel and slice the aubergines into rings, cover them with salt and place them between two plates and leave to draw for twenty minutes. Rinse them well in running water and pat dry with a cloth. Dip the slices into seasoned flour and then very quickly into a bowl of beer and then fry them in hot oil until they are brown on both sides. Drain them on some absorbent paper and arrange them in a dish. Pour over them a sauce made of yogurt with a little chopped garlic. Eat immediately.

**Ciğer Tavası** FRIED LIVER

½ *lb sheep's liver*
1 *tablespoon paprika*
2 *tablespoons flour*
1 *medium onion*
3 *sprigs parsley*
2 *tablespoons olive oil*
*Salt and pepper*

Wash and dry the liver and cut it into small pieces. Put the paprika into a saucer and roll the liver well into it and then dip the liver into seasoned flour and fry quickly in very hot oil; be careful not to overcook the liver as this will spoil the flavour. Arrange the pieces on a dish and sprinkle with some rock salt and finely chopped parsley and slices of raw onion.

**Pastırma** SPICED BEEF

This is a dried beef which has been highly flavoured with cummin, garlic and paprika. It can be obtained from the shops in the list at the front of the book. It has rather a strong spicy smell, is very delicious and is certainly extremely characteristic of Turkish food.

*Pastirma* can be served in several ways. As it comes, sliced very thin like salami; it can be fried like bacon; or it can be wrapped in buttered paper and baked in the oven for about twenty minutes.

# *Soup*

The distinction between a soup and a rather liquid stew is not very clearly marked in Turkish cooking. However, there are many good soups and broths to be had as well as those which almost make a meal in themselves. Borsch, which comes from the Balkans, now forms a part of the Turkish cuisine, as do vegetable purées, but there are many soups of purely Turkish origin.

Soups are usually served with lemon juice, which one squeezes on at table; this to my mind improves most soups just as a dash of sherry does many western soups. Fried croutons and fresh chopped mint are common garnishes, as well as yogurt and paprika. The Turks claim that metal spoons give a bad flavour to soup and they therefore prefer to eat it with wooden spoons, which are specially made by hand out of hardwood and are often beautifully carved.

**Et Suyu** MEAT STOCK

*Meat and bones from the neck, breast or shoulder of mutton, shin and knuckle of beef, ox-tail, sheep's head etc.*
*2 large onions*
*2 large or 3 small carrots*
*2 leeks*
*Salt*

Cover the bones and meat with cold water and bring it to the boil and keep removing the scum until the broth is clear, then add the vegetables and seasoning and simmer for two hours;

strain into a large bowl and cool and then skim off any fat. If the broth seems weak you can add a Maggi or Knorr cube and a pinch of monosodium glutamate is a great help.

**Tavuk Suyu** CHICKEN STOCK

*1 chicken (or the left-overs from a chicken together with the giblets)*
*1 large onion*
*3 sprigs parsley*
*Salt and pepper*

Cover the chicken with cold water and bring to the boil and remove all the scum that floats to the top; then add the onion and seasoning and simmer for one and a half hours. Strain the liquor into a bowl and allow it to cool and then skim off all the fat. This will make about one quart of stock.

**İşkembe Çorbası** TRIPE SOUP

*1 mutton tripe*
*1 lemon (rind and juice)*
*3 cloves garlic*
*1 oz butter*
*1 oz flour*
*½ pint milk*
*1 egg*
*1 tablespoon vinegar*
*Thyme*
*Marjoram*
*Paprika*
*Salt and pepper*

Wash the tripe very thoroughly under running water and then bring it rapidly to the boil in fresh cold water. Throw this water away. Cut the tripe up into very small strips and put it into a pot with two quarts of cold water, the rind of the lemon and the crushed garlic, season and add herbs and simmer for about two hours or until the tripe is tender. Skim off any froth that rises to the surface. Meanwhile, make a roux with the butter and flour. Add the milk, and then add the egg and lemon juice gradually; thin with a little of the tripe stock. Add this mixture to the tripe slowly, when the tripe is tender, and simmer again for about two minutes. Take off the heat, add the vinegar and some paprika and serve at once.

**Düğün Çorbası** WEDDING SOUP

*3 pints mutton, lamb, veal or beef broth*
*½ lb mince meat*
*Juice of 1 lemon*
*2 eggs*
*1 oz flour*
*½ oz butter*
*Paprika*
*Salt and pepper*

Prepare some tiny meat balls by mixing the mince with salt and pepper and one of the beaten eggs. Form into balls about the size of a hazel nut and throw these into the boiling broth. Meanwhile beat the remaining egg with the lemon juice and add the flour gradually until it is smooth. Take the soup off the boil and gradually add in the lemon mixture. Do *not* boil again as this will curdle the egg. In order to serve it hot, re-heat it carefully if necessary. Melt the butter and mix into it a teaspoon of paprika and decorate each bowl of soup with it just before serving.

**Manti Çorbası: 'Mantı' Soup from Adana**

The *manti* for this soup are prepared in the same way as the *mantı* I have described in the meat section except that for the soup the pastry is folded into little bags by squeezing it together at the top after the stuffing has been put in; any left-overs from the main *manti* dish would be ideal for the soup.

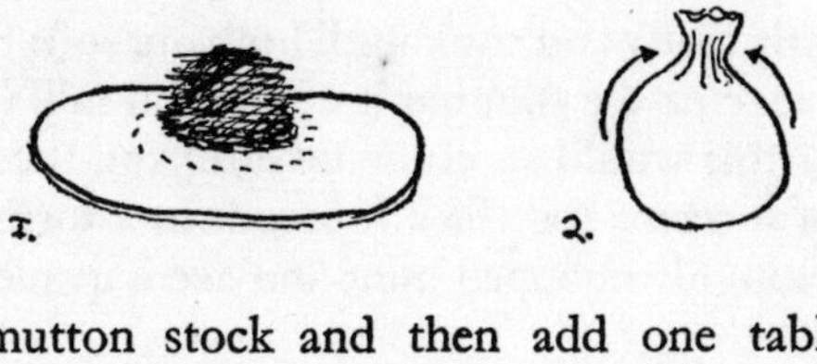


Prepare a mutton stock and then add one tablespoon of

chick peas to the stock and simmer them until they are soft.

If you are using fresh *mantı*, they should be simmered in the same stock for fifteen minutes, but if you are warming up some left-over *mantı* then they need only be warmed up in the soup. Make a fresh tomato purée and pour it into the soup just before serving.

The chick peas could be omitted in this soup as they merely serve to thicken it a bit; the *mantı* are just as good in a clear broth. A yogurt sauce can also be used instead of the tomatoes if preferred.

For the method of preparing *mantı* see page 61.

**Bezelye Çorbası** SPLIT PEA SOUP

*½ lb split peas*
1 *oz margarine*
1 *medium onion*
*½ lb spinach or one small tin*
1 *medium carrot*
1 *bay leaf*
*A few mint leaves*
*A little milk*
*Salt and pepper*

Soak the peas overnight and drain them and put them into two quarts of fresh water with a pinch of salt and bring to the boil and continue to boil gently. Meanwhile fry the roughly sliced onion and carrot in a little margarine for a few minutes and when the margarine is absorbed add them to the peas together with the bay leaf and seasoning and simmer until the peas are soft. Put in the washed and roughly chopped spinach when the peas are nearly ready and cook until both are soft. Pass the soup through a sieve or the thin mesh of a mouli mill (do not use a liquidizer as this would spoil the texture) and then thin with a little milk if it seems too thick. Serve it in a tureen, sprinkled with some roughly chopped mint and accompanied by a bowl of yogurt.

**Borç** BORSCH SOUP

*2 pints meat stock*
*2 medium onions*
*3 large beetroot*
*½ celeriac or celery*
*3 medium potatoes*
*2 skinned tomatoes*
*1 medium cabbage*
*1 square green pepper*
*3 cloves garlic*
*2 ozs margarine*
*Juice of 1 lemon*
*1 bay leaf*
*A few crushed dill seeds*
*3 or 4 sprigs parsley*
*Some chopped parsley*
*½ pint yogurt or sour cream*

Cut the onions, celery, potatoes and pepper into very small pieces and fry them in the margarine for a few minutes in the bottom of a strong pot and then add the skinned tomatoes, crushed garlic, shredded cabbage, grated beetroot and the stock; season well and put in the herbs (whole) and simmer until the vegetables are tender. Pour the soup into a warmed tureen, stir in the lemon juice and sprinkle with finely chopped parsley. Serve very hot accompanied by a bowl of thick yogurt or sour cream.

NOTE Borsch is traditionally served with the vegetables as they are in the soup, but it can be put through the medium mesh of a mouli mill and be served as a purée.

**Kuzu Ciğer Çorbası** LIVER SOUP

*½ lb lamb's liver*
*1 bunch spring onions*
*2 ozs butter*
*1 lb tomatoes*
*1 quart meat broth*
*1 clove garlic*
*Salt and pepper*

Melt one ounce of butter and fry the liver gently on both sides and then remove it as soon as the blood comes to the surface; cut it up into tiny pieces about the size of a pea and put aside. Cut the spring onions into quarter-inch sections and fry them gently in the bottom of a strong pot in the rest of the butter until they become a bright green; add the skinned tomatoes, broth and seasoning and bring gently to the boil; then add the liver and crushed garlic and simmer half an hour. Pour the soup into a tureen and decorate with a melted butter and paprika dressing.

**Balık Çorbası** FISH SOUP

*1 lb of any white fish*
*1 tablespoon flour*
*1 oz margarine*
*1 egg*
*1 lemon*
*1 bay leaf*
*2 or 3 sprigs parsley*
*Salt and pepper*

Cut the fish up roughly and simmer it in two and a half pints of water together with the bay leaf and seasoning. In a separate pan make a roux with the flour and margarine and add a little of the fish stock, add the beaten egg, and finally the rest of the stock until it is a smooth soup. Bone the fish, lay it in a soup tureen and pour the soup over it. Add the roughly chopped parsley and serve with wedges of lemon.

**Koyun Et Suyu** MUTTON BROTH

*2 lbs neck or best end of neck or shoulder of mutton or lamb*
*2 large onions*
*2 leeks*
*3 medium potatoes*
*1 oz margarine*
*2 or 3 sprigs parsley*
*Black pepper*
*Salt and pepper*

Fry the meat and bones for a few minutes in a little margarine in a large strong soup pot and then add two quarts of water and bring it to the boil; skim off any foam and wait until the water is clear before adding the vegetables and seasoning. Simmer for one and a half hours and then strain off the broth; put the vegetables and a little of the meat in a soup tureen and pour the broth over them together with a generous amount of chopped parsley and black pepper. A little yogurt stirred into this soup is also very good.

**Mercimek Çorbası** RED LENTIL SOUP

*2 quarts good beef stock*
*½ lb red lentils*
*2 medium onions*
*1 oz margarine*
*1 teaspoon paprika*
*1 bay leaf*
*Salt and pepper*
*Parsley, mint*

Slice the onions very fine and fry them in the margarine in a strong pot; when they start to soften add the washed lentils and stir them into the margarine for a few minutes and then pour in the stock, bay leaf, paprika and seasoning and simmer until the lentils are quite soft. Remove the bay leaf, sieve the soup and serve it very hot garnished with chopped parsley and mint.

**Yayla Çorbası** PLATEAU SOUP

This soup is eaten on the Anatolian plateau where the barley grows.

*½ lb barley*
*3 pints of any strong meat stock*
*1 medium onion*
*½ pint yogurt*
*3 or 4 sprigs parsley*
*A few mint leaves*
*Salt and pepper*

Soak the barley for a few hours until it is softened. Bring the stock to the boil and add the barley, the finely chopped onion and plenty of seasoning and continue to boil gently until the barley is cooked. Just before serving, draw the pot off the heat and stir in the yogurt. Serve at once sprinkled with roughly chopped parsley and mint.

**Şehriyeli Çorba** VERMICELLI SOUP

*¼ lb vermicelli*
*3 or 4 sprigs parsley*

*4 pints strong clear chicken or beef stock*
*Juice of 1 lemon*
*Salt and pepper*

It is very important that this soup is made with a good, rich stock. Season the stock well and bring it to the boil and add the vermicelli which should boil until tender. Squeeze the lemon juice into the broth just before serving and garnish with the finely chopped parsley. This pleasant soup is eaten everywhere but is often spoilt by being too watery.

**Tavuk Çorbası Yoğurtlu** CHICKEN SOUP WITH YOGURT

*3 pints chicken stock*
*2 ozs rice*
*½ pint yogurt*
*1 egg*
*3 or 4 sprigs parsley*
*A few mint leaves*
*Salt and pepper*

Simmer the rice in the chicken broth until tender and season the broth well. Mix the yogurt with the beaten egg and add a little of the broth to them bit by bit until well mixed; then gradually add to the rest of the stock, having drawn the pot off the heat so that it will not boil again, as this would curdle the egg. Heat very carefully to avoid boiling and serve at once with finely chopped mint and parsley.

**Domatesli Tavuk Suyu** CHICKEN AND TOMATO SOUP

*2 pints of chicken stock*
*1 pint tomato juice (or a purée made from fresh tomatoes)*
*½ a celeriac or celery*
*2 cloves garlic*
*1 medium onion*
*Juice of 1 lemon*
*3 sprigs parsley*
*Salt and pepper*

Bring the chicken broth to the boil and add the tomato juice or purée, together with the finely chopped onion, crushed garlic and diced celery. Season well and simmer until all are tender.

Pass the soup through a large-meshed sieve or a medium mouli mill. Serve the soup garnished with finely chopped parsley and with the lemon juice squeezed over it.

# *Fish*

The immensely long Turkish coastline, which includes the Black Sea, the Aegean and the Mediterranean, affords Turkey a vast variety of fish and sea food. Istanbul, situated on the Bosphorus, benefits from the seasonal flow of fish between the cool waters of the Black Sea and the warmer Sea of Marmara, and claims to have the tastiest fish of all. Whilst the coastal ports have fresh cheap fish all the year round, the inland towns, dependent on transport, are not so favoured and have to rely on a short supply which is often expensive.

Among the many species available, the swordfish is perhaps the most delicious and it is in season during September, October and November. The *lufer*, bluefish, red and grey mullet, bass and tuna are excellent among numerous others. Fresh prawns, shrimps, mussels, lobster, squid and octopus are always available, and caviar, salmon and trout are comparatively cheap in the north.

The best method, in my opinion, of cooking fish is to grill it over a charcoal fire and this is just what the Turks do best. The fish is either split open or cut into steaks, brushed with olive oil, placed on an oiled grid over the fire and quickly browned on both sides. It is then eaten immediately with plenty of lemon juice and rock salt. Other popular dishes are the cold fish stews called *Pilâki*, which are delightful, and the many baked recipes. The stuffed fish dishes I find rather fussy, although they do add variety to the menu.

The floating restaurants in Istanbul are famous for their sea

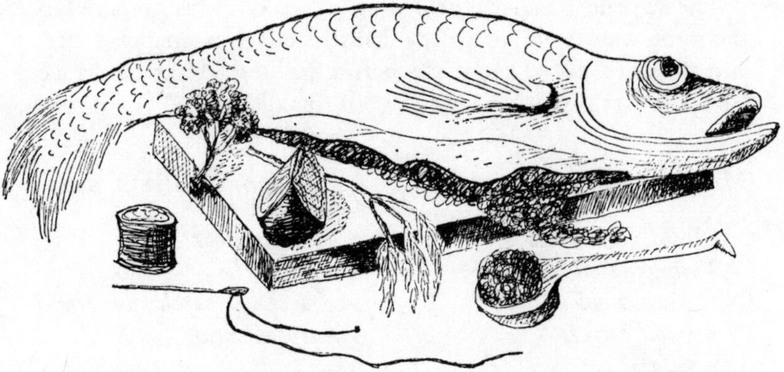

food. They are situated near the Galata Bridge and as one threads one's way between the charcoal fires, the indescribable smell of grilling fish wafts through the air. When you finally choose your table floating at the water's edge, you can select your fresh fish and it is then cooked in front of you and served hot with lemon and parsley, with perhaps a salad or a hot pepper and a huge hunk of bread. This, with a glass of tea, is perhaps one of the most perfect meals possible. The smell of the sea front and the sight of little boats ploughing their way up and down the Golden Horn all add a charm and delight of their own, and enhance an already perfect meal.

**Kılıc Izgarada** GRILLED SWORDFISH

Grilled swordfish is considered one of the specialities of Turkish cooking and owes its fame to the particularly delicious flavour of the swordfish which breeds around the Turkish coast.

The fish is cut into thick slices, marinated in a mixture of paprika, lemon juice, olive oil, onion juice and salt, and is left to steep for three or four hours before cooking. The bars of the grill are oiled and the fish is grilled quickly on both sides and eaten immediately with a lemon sauce.

The swordfish is often grilled on *şiş* sticks and is prepared in the same way as above except that it is cut into smaller cubes, and threaded on to the sticks before grilling. A tarator sauce (see pages 134–5) is very good with this dish.

**Midye Pilâkisi** COLD MUSSEL STEW

*About* 30 *mussels*
½ *cup olive oil*
2 *medium onions*
2 *small carrots*
1 *potato*
1 *celery or celeriac*
2 *large tomatoes*
4 *cloves garlic*
*A few sprigs parsley and fennel*
1 *teaspoon sugar*
*Salt*

Wash and scrub the mussels thoroughly and rinse them in plenty of water until all the sand is removed. Put them very wet into a strong pot with a lid and cook them as they are until the shells open; no further water is needed. Shake the pot from time to time while they are steaming. Save any liquor and add it to the stew.

Prepare all the vegetables except the tomatoes by cutting them up fairly small and frying them in the olive oil until they become a little softer; then add the skinned tomatoes, a teaspoon of sugar, salt, fennel and a cup of water and continue to simmer them until they are tender. Now lie the mussels on top of the vegetables and cook for a further five minutes. Allow them to cool in the pot and serve with chopped parsley and lemon juice.

**Uskumru Papaz Yahnisi** COLD MACKEREL

1 *mackerel for each person*
3 *tablespoons olive oil*
3 *medium onions*
3 *medium carrots*
4 *cloves garlic*
¼ *pint tomato purée or juice*
1 *teaspoon paprika*
3 *sprigs parsley*
1 *lemon*
*Salt and pepper*

Wash and clean the mackerel; cut the heads off and scrape off all the scales by rubbing a knife from the tail to the head until the skin is clear. Clean the fish and make three small incisions across the back where the flesh is thickest. Wipe dry.

Parboil the onions and carrots and then chop them up roughly. Put the olive oil into a baking pan and spread the onions and carrots all over it so that they form a flat bed on to which you can lay the mackerel side by side. Add the crushed garlic, tomato purée, sprigs of parsley, seasoning and two cups of water. Cover with tinfoil paper and bake in a moderate oven (350) for half an hour, or until the mackerel are done, which will be when the flesh separates easily from the bone and is no longer pink. Allow the fish to cool in the pan and serve as they are with wedges of lemon and fresh bread.

**Balık Köftesi** FISH BALLS

- 2 *large haddock fillets together weighing about* 1½ *lbs*
- 2 *thick slices old white bread*
- 1 *medium onion, grated*
- 1 *egg*
- 1 *oz cornflour*
- 4 *sprigs parsley*
- *Salt and pepper*
- *Olive oil for deep frying*

Remove all the bones from the fillets and then take hold of the skin by the tail end and scrape off all the flesh with a sharp knife. It will come off quite easily if you scrape from tail to head. Put the flesh into a mortar and pound it well until it becomes quite broken up and mushey; when it is all pounded put it into a basin and mix it with the crumbled dry bread, onion, egg, finely chopped parsley and seasoning and knead them all thoroughly together until the mixture feels quite smooth. Add the flour if it feels too wet to handle properly. Form into little balls the size of a walnut which can either be dropped into a boiling broth or rolled in egg and fried in hot oil.

**Midye Dolması** STUFFED MUSSELS

| | |
|---|---|
| *About* 30 *mussels* | 2 *ozs currants* |
| ½ *cup dry rice* | 1 *oz sugar* |
| 2 *medium onions* | 1 *pint stock* |
| 2 *ozs pine nuts* | 3 *or* 4 *sprigs parsley* |

Wash and scrape the mussels thoroughly and rinse in plenty of water. Force them open and remove the beard (see page 33) and any black bits with a pair of scissors but do not remove the mussel itself from the shell. Leave in slightly salty water.

Meanwhile prepare the stuffing. Fry the finely chopped onions in two tablespoons of olive oil and then add the nuts, currants, sugar, finely chopped parsley, seasoning and the washed rice and enough stock to just cover them. Cook out all the liquid and then cool the mixture.

Now take each mussel and put a teaspoon of the stuffing inside the open shell, close it and tie firmly with cotton. When they are all ready, pack them firmly into a pot and press them down with an inverted saucer; add a pint and a half of boiling water and simmer, covered, for half an hour: then strain off the water and allow them to cool. Serve the mussels with a tarator sauce (see pages 134–5).

**Balık Fırın** BAKED WHOLE FISH

Any large fish such as silverfish, bass, mullet, pomfret, cod, halibut, salmon or turbot could be cooked this way.

After cleaning and wiping the fish, lie it whole in a large baking pan with just enough water to prevent it drying out, and add two ounces of butter, a teaspoon of salt and a broken bay leaf. Bake it very gently in a moderate oven (350) until it is done, which will be when the flesh separates from the bone easily and is loose. Be very careful not to over-cook the fish as this will spoil the delicate flavour. The time it will take depends on the size of the fish and the only reliable method of gauging it is to keep testing the fish as it cooks. Serve it whole with a lemon or tarator sauce (see pages 134–5).

**Kilıc Domatesli** SWORDFISH WITH TOMATOES

Any white fish can be cooked like this, although the swordfish has a unique flavour.

1 *lb swordfish*
4 *tomatoes*
2 *tablespoons olive oil*
*Lemon juice*
*A pinch dry basil*
3 *or* 4 *sprigs parsley*
1 *bay leaf*
*Salt and pepper*

Skin the fish and cut it into thick slices and arrange them in a baking tin side by side.

Simmer the skinned tomatoes in the olive oil with a little salt until they become soft; then add the herbs and a squeeze of lemon juice. Pour the sauce over the fish so that it is all covered and then bake very gently in a moderate oven (350) for about twenty minutes or until it is just done which will be when the flesh is loose. Allow the fish to cool in its tray and serve cold.

**Uskumru Dolması** STUFFED MACKEREL

This is another of the stuffed dishes for which the Turks seem to have such a partiality. It is a bit tricky at first to get the knack of pulling all the flesh out of the mackerel without breaking the skin. The head and tail are not removed and you have to clean the fish as best you can through a small opening just under the head. After breaking the back bone in several places by bending it, you rock the fish backwards and forwards with your finger tips until all the flesh has been loosened from the skin and can be pulled out through the little hole under the head. The flesh is then cooked with the stuffing and repacked into the fish to form its original shape once again!

*Allow one fish for each person*

For the stuffing:

*2 medium onions*
*Butter for frying*
*2 tablespoons pine nuts*
*A pinch cinnamon*
*2 ozs currants*
*3 or 4 sprigs parsley*
*Egg*
*Flour*
*Salt and pepper*
*Lemon*
*Olive oil for frying*

Sauté the finely sliced onions in about a tablespoon of butter until they are transparent. Add the cut up flesh of the fish and all the other ingredients and continue to fry gently together, stirring lightly. Allow the stuffing to cool a little before packing it carefully back into the skin of the mackerel. Roll the fish carefully in beaten egg and seasoned flour and fry them in oil until they are brown on both sides. Serve hot with lemon wedges.

## Sebzeli Levrek — BASS WITH VEGETABLES

*1 bass, mullet or cod cut into steaks*
*2 large potatoes*
*4 medium carrots*
*1 celery or celeriac*
*4 cloves garlic*
*Juice of 1 lemon*
*3 or 4 sprigs parsley*

Cut the vegetables up into pieces and put them into a large pot together with the crushed garlic and seasoning and add enough water to just cover them; simmer until they start to become soft. Lay the fish steaks on top of the vegetables, cover the pot, and continue cooking very gently until the fish is just done. It will be spoilt if it is allowed to over-cook. Arrange the steaks on a serving dish, carefully, with the vegetables around and sprinkle with chopped parsley and lemon juice.

**Barbunya** STEAMED RED MULLET

*As many fish as required (they should be small ones)*
½ *cup olive oil*
1 *cup water*
*Small bunch dill*
3 *sprigs parsley*
*Juice of* 1 *lemon*
*Salt and pepper*

Wash the fish and clean them and remove all the scales. Arrange them side by side in a large frying pan which can be covered. Pour the olive oil and the water over the fish, lay the unchopped herbs around them, and season well. Cover the pan and heat gently for about ten minutes, or until the flesh is loose. Allow the fish to cool in the pan or transfer them to a serving dish. Serve them cold with the juice of one lemon squeezed over them.

NOTE Small herrings could be used in this dish and it makes a very useful start to a meal. These cold dishes are very popular in Turkey during the summer.

**Balık Pilâki** FISH STEW

1½ *lbs any large white fish*
2 *large tomatoes*
2 *or* 3 *cloves garlic*
1 *bay leaf*
2 *or* 3 *sprigs parsley*
½ *cup olive oil*
*Salt and pepper*
*Lemon*

Clean, bone and skin the fish and cut into pieces of about two inches square. Make an incision with a sharp knife into the side of each piece and insert a slice of garlic and a little bit of the broken bay leaf. Arrange them in a wide baking pan and lay the sliced skinned tomatoes over the top. Season them well and sprinkle some finely chopped parsley over them and pour over all the olive oil. Add just enough water to cover the bottom of the pan and bake them in a slow oven (300) until they are done, which will be when the flesh is loose and separates easily. This dish can be eaten hot but is usually allowed to cool in its pan. Serve with wedges of lemon.

**Haslanmiş İstakoz** LOBSTERS

In Turkey lobsters are sold alive and this necessitates the unpleasant business of cooking them. Prepare any large pot of fast boiling salty water and drop the lobster into it and boil for twenty minutes, then remove him from the water and allow to cool. In spite of its gruesome aspects this does ensure a much fresher and tastier lobster. Break off the claws and crack them so that the flesh can be removed easily, then turn the lobster upside down and cut open the under side from head to tail and remove the veins, sac, and any spongy material near the head. Pull the shell open and pour a little lemon juice, olive oil and seasoning on to the flesh and serve cold.

**İzgarada İstakoz** GRILLED LOBSTER

After cooking the lobster as described above, take out all the flesh, chop it up and mix it with some lemon juice, a little roughly chopped parsley, cream, salt and pepper, and return it to the shell; sprinkle bread crumbs on top and dot with butter and then grill for a few minutes until the top is brown.

**Fırında Mezit** BAKED HADDOCK

8 *haddock fillets*
2 *cups cooked rice*
4 *hard boiled eggs*
2 *ozs butter*
*Breadcrumbs to cover the fillets*
3 *or* 4 *sprigs parsley*
*Lemon*
*Salt and pepper*

Mix the rice, chopped eggs and finely chopped parsley together. Lay four fillets on the bottom of a greased baking dish and spread the mixture over them; lay the other four fillets on top, dot with butter and cover with bread crumbs; add a little water and bake them in a moderate oven (350) for about twenty-five minutes. Serve with lemon wedges.

**Kağıtta Balik Buğulaması** FISH COOKED IN PAPER

*As many boneless fillets as persons*
*Butter as required*
2 *tablespoons grated onion*
3 *or* 4 *sprigs parsley*
*Lemon juice*
*Greaseproof paper*
*Olive oil*
*Salt and pepper*

Cut the fillets into serving size pieces and allow enough paper to wrap each piece in a double layer of paper. Dampen the greaseproof paper and then brush it well with olive oil; place a piece of fish on each sheet and add a teaspoon of butter, a little onion, half a sprig of parsley and seasoning; gather up the paper at the top and tie securely so that nothing will be able to run out. Place the bundles in some boiling water and cook for fifteen minutes; remove from the water, carefully untie the string, slide the fish out on to a serving dish and pour any juice over it. Serve with pepper and wedges of lemon.

**Levrek Fırın** STUFFED BASS

*A cod or bass of about* 4 *lbs weight*
*Salt*
*Lemon juice*

For the stuffing:
1 *tablespoon grated onion*
½ *cup chopped celery or celeriac*
1 *tablespoon parsley*
1 *cup bread crumbs*
1 *oz butter*
1 *lemon*
*Salt and pepper*

For the sauce:
1 *chopped onion*
1 *green pepper*
2 *cups tomato purée*
*Butter*
*Lemon juice*
*A few sprigs parsley*
*Salt and pepper*

Clean and bone the fish without cutting it right through; wipe it well and rub salt and lemon juice into the skin.

Prepare the stuffing by frying the onion, celery and the roughly chopped parsley in the butter until they are soft, and then stirring in the bread crumbs and seasoning and the juice of one lemon. Allow it to cool a little before stuffing it into the fish and then sew up the side of the fish that was opened. Place the fish on a buttered dish and bake in a moderate oven (350) until it is done, which is when the flesh separates easily. Meanwhile make a sauce by lightly frying the chopped onion in a little more butter and then adding the tomato purée, the thinly sliced pepper, a few sprigs of parsley and a squeeze of lemon juice. Season the sauce well and pour over the fish just before serving.

# *Meat and Chicken*

The Turkish practice is to include, under the general heading of 'Vegetables', many dishes which also contain a fair proportion of meat, so when selecting a meat recipe one should also consult the 'Vegetable Dishes' section.

Lamb is perhaps the most common meat available in Turkey. It has a unique flavour which is said to be produced by the wild thyme which grows all over the steppe where the flocks graze, and renders the meat strong and spicy. I find it absolutely delicious, especially when young and tender. The mutton and goat are inclined to be rather tough and stringy. Veal is used quite a lot, especially in stews such as the *türlü*, but the beef is generally of a poor quality as the cattle are kept for draught work and dairy produce. It is important to note that in the mince, *köfte*, dishes (rissoles) RAW mince is always used. Chickens, rabbits and game are plentiful and good.

Cummin, paprika and yogurt are used a lot in the preparation of meat dishes and also for marinating them. Olive oil and lemon juice are also a common marinade, and most herbs are used, especially parsley and thyme.

**Kuzu Pirzolası** GRILLED LAMB CHOPS

These chops are delicious when young lamb is used, but are inclined to be rather tough if mutton is served.

The chops should be cut rather thin and then pounded well on a wooden board with a wooden mallet or other flat heavy instrument, until they are flattened and enlarged. (A rolling pin is a good substitute if you do not have a mallet.) Allow them to marinate for as long as possible in some olive oil, lemon juice, onions sliced in rings, salt and pepper.

It is very important that the grill is as hot as possible before starting to cook and that the meat is grilled quickly on both sides so that the outside is well browned and the inside still a little pink; in this way the meat remains tender. Most domestic grills do not get quite hot enough and this causes slower, tougher cooking. There is not really a substitute for the charcoal fire and the slightly smoky flavour that it imparts to the meat, but providing one starts with a good glow, the results

can be very satisfactory in the kitchen. Now that outdoor barbecues are becoming so popular, one could get much of the authentic Turkish effect, providing that real charcoal is used. Artificial charcoal sold for barbecues and wood fires does not give the same effect as real charcoal. When the fire is getting red, throw a little salt over it, which will reduce the smoke and keep it glowing while one is cooking.

### Şiş Kebab — SKEWERED LAMB

This dish gets its name from the Turkish word *şiş* which means stick. These sticks are long flattened iron skewers pointed at one end and thicker at the other, on to which the meat is threaded. The flattened shape prevents the meat from twisting round when it is being grilled over a fire. About six pieces of meat are threaded on one stick and most households would have at least eight *şiş* sticks available for grilling when required. Each stick is about two feet long.

It is essential to use young lamb and the cut is usually taken from the leg. Bone the meat and cut it into little cubes which should be marinated for as long as possible, overnight being ideal. Put them into a bowl with sliced onions, olive oil, lemon juice and plenty of salt and pepper, and leave in a cool place.

When ready for cooking, heat the grill or fire to as hot as possible, and then thread the meat on the oiled sticks and grill as quickly as possible so that the outside is well browned, but the inside still slightly pink. When they are ready, push the pieces of meat off the sticks on to a warm plate and sprinkle with rock salt and thyme and eat at once.

Accompanied by a tomato salad and some bread, *şiş kebab*, to my mind, is perhaps the most perfect meal possible and I like to think of the countless generations of shepherds who discovered this simple way of eating lamb.

*Siş kebabs* are never served on the stick and therefore one is never faced with that awful problem of how to eat them that sometimes arises at dinner parties, especially when one is tackling little pieces of warmed-up leather; these horrors bear no relationship to the tender melting *kebabs* in Turkey.

**Tandır Kebab** WHOLE LAMB DISHES

At weddings or special religious festivals called *bayram* days, and especially at the end of *Ramadan*, which is the Muslim fasting month similar to Lent, a whole lamb might well be cooked and many people will join together to enjoy the feast. There are several methods of cooking whole sheep or lamb and they are interesting to note, even if one seldom has the opportunity of trying them out oneself.

The *tandır kebab* is an Anatolian dish. A wide shallow pit is prepared and a bed of hot charcoal is spread out in the pit. The carcass of the sheep, together with potatoes in their skins, is laid on the hot coals and the whole is then completely covered over with earth and the meat is left to bake slowly for several hours. When it is considered ready, the carcass is removed from the earth, brushed to get rid of any soil and then held over a huge brass tray and shaken vigorously until all the meat falls off into the tray. Salt, thyme and black pepper are sprinkled over the meat and it is then eaten right away with everyone helping themselves with their hands. A good greasy time is had by all. Large trays of pilaf, salads, yogurt and white bread would, of course, accompany such a meal, as well as a sticky sweet such as *tel kadayıf* and plenty of strong black coffee.

Another interesting method, used around the Black Sea coast, is the *piran* (the word means 'a hole'). This time a deep vertical hole is dug about three feet wide and five feet deep and a fire is laid at the bottom of the pit. The lamb is inserted lengthwise into the hole and the top covered over and it then cooks for three or four hours and the result is very much the same as in the *tandır kebab*.

Lamb and sheep are also roasted over a hot fire on a spit and turned around slowly or they can be stuffed and baked in the ovens of the local baker. The meat is larded with little pieces of garlic and the stuffing consists of rice, onions, nuts, currants and herbs and is packed into the carcass and securely sewn up before roasting. The meat is usually very well done and should fall off the bone.

**Mantı** ANCIENT DISH SIMILAR TO RAVIOLI

This is a very interesting meat dish which has probably originated in Central Asia and has travelled west with the movement of the nomads. It is the national dish of Mongolia and is certainly related to the Mant'ou, a family of steamed stuffed breads of Chinese origin. I was particularly interested to discover it in Turkey. It is the type of food that can be prepared in quantity and then heated up at a later time and is therefore ideal for a nomadic people, or shepherds far from home, who can thus provide themselves with a hot meal quickly and in difficult conditions.

½ *lb flour (this will make about 35 mantı)*
1 *egg*
*Salt*
*Cold water*

For the stuffing:
1 *lb minced lamb*
1 *large onion*
4 *or* 5 *sprigs parsley*
1 *egg*
*Black pepper and salt*

To make the dough: Put the flour into a large basin with the salt and break the egg into the centre, adding just enough cold water to make a dough. Knead this very well and leave aside. Make the stuffing by grating the onion into the mince, together with the finely chopped parsley, the seasoning and egg, and squeeze well with your hand until it is smoothly mixed. Now roll out the dough with plenty of flour on the table until it is as large as possible and as thin as can be handled without breaking. Use a long thin stick for this and you will find it much easier to manage.

Now cut little squares of pastry, put a teaspoon of meat on to them, and fold over, sealing the edges well with water. They

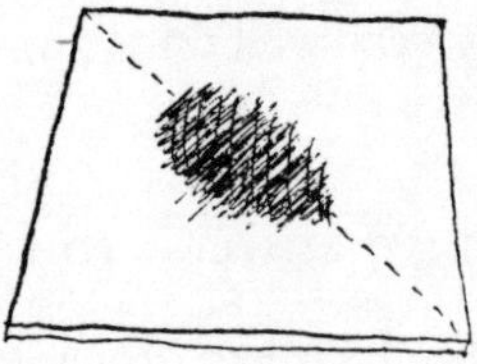

1.

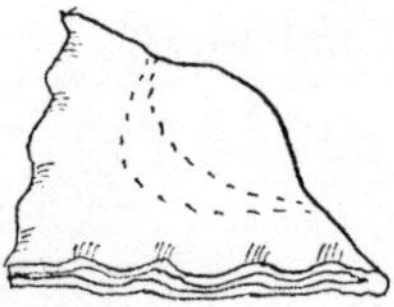

2.

should be about one and a half inches square. Lay them out on a floured cloth until all are ready. Prepare a large pot of boiling salted water and drop the *mantı* into it carefully and boil gently for about twenty minutes. Lift them out with a drainer and put them into a colander and rinse them well under cold running water. At this stage they can be kept until they are needed or they can be stored in the refrigerator for several days.

To serve, return the *mantı* to the pot, add just enough broth to cover and simmer gently until they are hot. Put them on to a warm serving dish and pour either a good tomato sauce or a yogurt and garlic sauce over them. To make the tomato sauce, simmer several skinned, roughly chopped tomatoes in butter with a little crushed garlic, basil, salt and black pepper. To make the yogurt sauce add a little chopped garlic to yogurt.

*Mantı* are very filling and make a meal in themselves. The busy Turkish cook makes a quantity which can be used over a period of time.

**Döner Kebab** MEAT ON A VERTICAL SPIT

*The döner kebab is a famous Turkish speciality which is seen everywhere and although it would be impracticable for home use, is never-*

*theless interesting enough to mention; no book on Turkish food would be complete without it.*

The meat, in this intriguing dish, is wrapped around a large vertical spit and grilled in front of an ingenious tier of charcoal fires which are on shelves one above the other. In this way the huge kebab is cooked as it slowly turns, emitting a delicious smell which informs the passers-by that the *döner kebab* is ready. These kebabs are usually only made in restaurants and the owner stands in his door and encourages one to step in and try his *döner kebab*.

The following method of preparing the *döner kebab* was

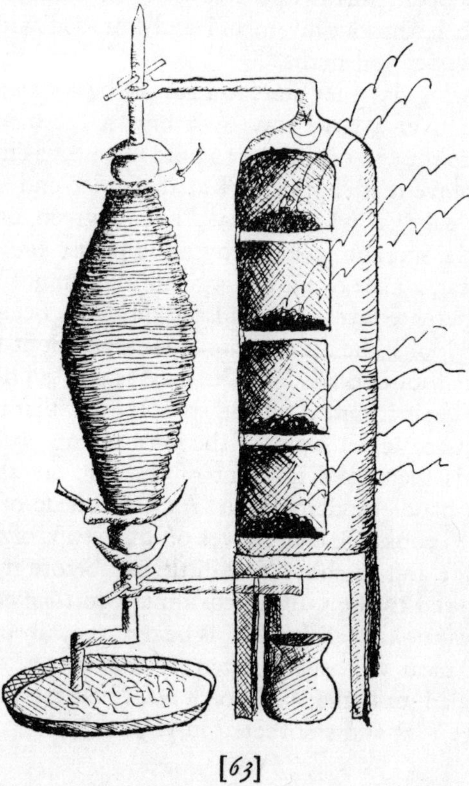

shown to me by a cook in Trabzon, whose *lokanta* was especially good. It takes twenty-four hours to prepare the *döner kebab* and so one starts each day to make the *döner* for the next day. At least a whole lamb will be used, together with the tail of the fat-tailed sheep, and about six pounds of minced lamb.

The meat, including the fat, is carefully boned and then cut into large slices about the size of a saucer. When enough of the meat is cut, it is then put into a very large basin and left to marinate for twenty-four hours in a mixture of olive oil, sliced onions, salt, tomatoes, thyme, sage, parsley, vinegar, yogurt and black pepper. Meanwhile a further six pounds or so of minced lamb is thoroughly mixed and kneaded with several eggs, salt, pepper and herbs.

The following day they start to load the heavy spit which is held upright over a large tray by a boy; a flat metal disc is fastened on to the end of the spit to hold the meat as it is loaded on and to prevent it slipping off at the other end. First, for appearances sake, a whole tomato and a green pepper are speared on the spit and pushed down to the disc end, and then a slice of meat, a slice of fat and a handful of mince; these are loaded in alternate layers until all the meat has been used up and the spit looks like an enormous sausage about three feet long and one foot in diameter. The meat is pressed down hard and the outside is trimmed off and smoothed so that it is nicely rounded and the actual layers of the meat are not visible.

The spit is then fixed in front of the braziers and slowly turned by a handle underneath it. As the outside of the *döner kebab* starts to cook, the chef shaves off thin strips of meat with a special knife and catches it in a little pan before it falls, and these are served to the waiting customers: in this way a fresh part is always cooking as the *döner* is being gradually consumed. The bits of meat are usually eaten by themselves with some bread and salad, or perhaps laid on a *pide* (see Pastry and Bread section, page 112) and smothered in yogurt.

**Talaş Kebab** MEAT PASTRY ROLL

1 *lb plain flour*
2 *eggs*
1 *tablespoon yogurt*
1 *tablespoon olive oil*
*Salt*
8 *ozs butter or margarine*

For the filling:
1 *lb lamb*
3 *large tomatoes*
1 *oz butter*
3 *or* 4 *sprigs parsley*
*Salt and pepper*

Sift the flour into a large bowl and make a well in the centre and into this break the eggs and add the olive oil, yogurt and a little salt. With a wooden spoon gradually work the liquids into the flour using a circular motion around the edge of the bowl until a dough starts to form; then knead with your hand for about five minutes until it is soft and pliable. Put the dough on to a floured surface and roll it out until it is about a quarter of an inch thick, then dot little bits of butter about the size of a small grape all over it and fold it up from end to end and side to side and roll it out again. Repeat this process three more times until all the eight ounces of butter have been used up. Put aside in a cool place.

To prepare the filling, cut the lamb into small cubes and fry it gently in one ounce of butter until it is brown all over, then add the skinned tomatoes, finely chopped parsley and seasoning and continue to simmer until all the liquid has cooked out. Cool before using.

Divide the pastry into half and roll out each half into a long piece about seven inches wide and as long as it will go. Put half the filling at the end of each piece and roll them up like a Swiss roll; moisten the ends and close them up. Put the rolls into a greased baking dish and brush them over with melted butter and bake them in a hot oven (400) for forty minutes or until they are nicely browned. Serve them with a tomato sauce (see page 136) in a separate bowl.

**Parça Kuşlar** MINCE WRAPPED IN SLICES OF LAMB

This dish is supposed to come from Gaziantep and is considered one of the tastiest ways of preparing meat in Turkey!

- 8 *pieces of lamb about* 3 *ins by* 3 *ins, cut* very *thin for wrapping*
- 1 *lb minced lamb*
- 1 *medium onion*
- 2 *tomatoes*
- *Salt and pepper*

Slice the onion very thinly and fry it in some butter until transparent and then add the mince; stir until it becomes dry and then add the skinned and roughly chopped tomatoes, season well and continue frying it until it is almost dry. Allow the meat to cool slightly and then form it into little sausages about the size of one finger. Now wrap each sausage in a piece of the thin lamb and secure it with a toothpick. Arrange all the bundles in a baking pan. Add just enough water to cover the bottom of the pan and bake for one hour in a moderate oven (350). Take them out of their pan and put them into a warm serving dish and pour over them a parsley and lemon sauce (page 133).

**Türlü** RICH STEW

- 2 *lbs veal, mutton or lamb (these meats can be used together)*
- 2 *pints stock (or water)*
- 2 *large onions*
- 4 *medium potatoes*
- 2 *large tomatoes*
- 2 *good-sized aubergines either round or long*
- 1 *large green capsicum*
- 1 *medium marrow or* 2 *courgettes*
- 4 *ozs okra*
- 4 *ozs French beans*
- 3 *or* 4 *cloves garlic*
- 3 *sprigs parsley*
- *Pinch of dry basil*
- 1 *bay leaf*
- 1 *teaspoon paprika*
- 4 *ozs butter*
- *Salt and pepper*

Slice the aubergines, salt them well, place them between two plates and leave aside. Cut the meat into large pieces and brown it well in two ounces of butter in a large strong stew pot. Cut all the other vegetables into reasonable sizes and add them to the meat (keeping back the aubergines). Stir the vegetables into the butter for a few minutes and then pour in about two pints of water or stock, season well and add the herbs whole. Now rinse the aubergines, pat them dry and then fry them on both sides in two ounces of butter in a separate pan and add to the stew together with the paprika. Cover the pot and simmer for about two hours or put into a slow oven (300).

This stew is eaten around Erzerum in the eastern part of Turkey where it is very cold in the winter: the seasonal vegetables being used when available.

### Yoğurtlu Kebab — MEAT WITH YOGURT

This is a particularly satisfying dish and is sometimes made with rissoles or with slices of meat taken from the *döner kebab*.

| | |
|---|---|
| 1 *lb lamb taken from the leg* | *Olive oil* |
| 2 *pides or slices of brown bread* | *Paprika* |
| 1 *pint yogurt* | *Melted butter* |
| 1 *onion* | *Salt and pepper* |

*Pides* (described in the special list on page 16) are used in this dish, but thick slices of brown bread could be substituted. Toast them and keep them warm.

Cut the meat into small cubes and marinate them in some olive oil, onion, salt and pepper for several hours. Heat some butter in a frying pan and fry the meat quickly so that it is brown all over, and lay it on top of the *pide* or toast, then pour over this the warm beaten yogurt. Stir some paprika powder into the hot browned butter that the meat was fried in and pour this over the yogurt and serve right away.

**Ciğer Yahnisi** LIVER STEW

This is a local dish from Manisa and is a very good way of disguising liver, should that be necessary.

*¾ lb sheep's liver*
2 *medium onions*
3 *large tomatoes*
*¾ lb washed rice*
2 *ozs butter*
2 *pints water*
*Salt and pepper*

Cut the liver up into small pieces about one inch square and sprinkle them with salt and pepper. Heat two ounces of butter in a large pot and gently fry the finely sliced onions until they become soft, but not brown. Add the skinned tomatoes and the liver and fry for a few minutes before adding the washed rice and the water. Season well and cook until the rice is tender. This is not strictly a pilaf and should be much wetter and more like a stew.

**Yarma Ekşili Dolma** LEAVES STUFFED WITH WHEAT IN A SAUCE

This dish comes from Malatya and consists of coarse-ground wheat flour called *yarma* made into a dough and wrapped up in edible leaves and served with a sauce.

8 *ozs yarma*
1 *teaspoon salt*
*Enough leaves for use (cherry, bean, apricot or vine leaves are all suitable)*

For the sauce:
3 *medium onions*
1 *pint yogurt*
*Juice of* 1 *lemon*
2 *ozs butter*

Put the *yarma* into a bowl with a teaspoon of salt and make a hole in the centre into which you should add just enough water to make a dough. Take out bits of the dough and roll into a little sausage the size of a finger and wrap this securely in a leaf. Pack the bundles firmly in a cooking pot, so that they cannot move about when they are being cooked; several layers will help to keep them in position. When they are all ready press an inverted saucer down on them and cover with warm water to just over their level. Simmer them for one hour with the lid on. (Quite a lot of the water will have been absorbed by the flour inside.)

Make the sauce by frying the onions in two ounces of butter until they are soft, but not brown, and then mix into them the yogurt, lemon juice and a little of the stock from the dolmas. Arrange the *dolmas* on a dish and pour this sauce over them.

**Etli Yaprak Dolması** STUFFED VINE LEAVES

1 *lb minced lamb*
2 *ozs butter*
4 *ozs rice*
*A small bunch dill*
1 *medium onion*
3 *or* 4 *sprigs parsley*
*Enough edible leaves*
*Lemon juice*
*Salt and pepper*

Vine leaves can usually be bought in tins in many countries, if you cannot obtain fresh ones. Cabbage is just as good and can always be substituted if necessary. If you are using fresh vine leaves, they should be boiled for a few minutes to soften them and the central vein should be cut out, dividing the leaf into two halves. Cabbage leaves should also be boiled for a few minutes before using.

To make the stuffing, cook the washed rice in a little butter and then cover with water and allow it to boil out and then cool. Mix the cooled rice into the mince together with the grated onion, finely chopped parsley, chopped dill, salt and pepper: these should all be very thoroughly kneaded together.

Spread out the vine leaves and put a teaspoon of the mixture onto each leaf and then fold them up into secure little packages. Pack them tightly into a pot, wedging them in, in layers, so that they cannot come undone during the cooking. Put an inverted saucer on top of the dolmas, add about a pint of water, two ounces of butter and a little lemon juice and cover tightly. Simmer for about an hour. When they are ready take them out, arrange them on a serving dish and serve with a bowl of yogurt.

**Maydanozlu Sulu Köfte** PARSLEY RISSOLES

| | |
|---|---|
| 1 *lb minced lamb or beef* | ½ *teaspoon black pepper* |
| 2 *medium onions* | 4 *ozs parsley* |
| 2 *ozs cooked rice* | 2 *ozs margarine* |
| 1 *egg* | *Salt and pepper* |

Wash and chop the parsley fairly finely and put it aside in a saucer. Grate the onions and add them to the mince together with the rice, egg and seasoning and knead them well; form them into small balls about the size of an egg, wet them slightly and then roll them in the parsley so that they are completely covered in it.

Prepare a pot of boiling water into which two ounces of margarine has been melted, and a half teaspoonful of salt, and carefully lower the balls into it . The parsley will not come off if the water is boiling all the time. Simmer them for twenty minutes and then take them out with a drainer and put them in a warm serving dish and pour a lemon sauce (page 133) over them.

**Güvec** EARTHENWARE CASSEROLES

*Güvec* can be made with meat and vegetables or just with vegetables. It is always baked in little individual earthenware dishes, which are served direct from the oven and one eats straight out of the casserole, usually with a bowl of yogurt. This is a very basic dish and popular for any meal, even breakfast.

| | |
|---|---|
| 2 *lb mutton, lamb or veal* | 2 *medium onions* |
| 3 *medium aubergines* | 4 *large potatoes* |

*½ lb green beans*
*3 large tomatoes*
*2 medium courgettes*
*2 ozs butter*
*Paprika*
*A pinch thyme*
*3 or 4 sprigs parsley*
*Salt and pepper*

This amount will make roughly four individual casseroles.

Peel and slice the aubergines and salt them for fifteen minutes before using.

Cut the meat into serving-size pieces, slice the onions roughly, quarter the potatoes, and halve the beans. Skin and quarter the tomatoes and cut the courgettes into slices. In one large frying pan brown the meat and onions in two ounces of butter and then divide them into the four casseroles adding equal amounts of vegetables to each dish. Rinse the aubergine slices and lay them over the top and add about two tablespoonfuls of water each, together with a broken sprig of parsley and of thyme. Bake them in a moderate oven (350) for forty-five minutes or until they are well cooked and brown on top.

*Güvec* could be made all in one large casserole and then divided before serving, but I feel it is best made in the way described, as this way saves any fuss just before the meal begins and looks nicer. Serve very hot with a pinch of paprika over each dish and a bowl of beaten yogurt.

**Konya Kebab** LAMB COOKED IN THE TRADITIONAL KONYA STYLE

This is a very delicious dish and is renowned all over Turkey, but for some reason it always tastes better when it is eaten in Konya!

*2 lbs spring lamb*
*½ lb spring onions*
*1 cos lettuce*
*3 large tomatoes*
*A few leaves mint*
*2 or 3 sprigs parsley*
*Salt and pepper*

For this dish the best-quality lamb should be used. Cut the meat into pieces about the size of a large chop and put them into an earthenware casserole with a well-fitting lid. The meat is baked without any water and the lid must be sealed with flour paste to prevent evaporation. Bake the meat just as it is for about two hours in a moderate oven (about 320) and then take it out and lay on top of the meat the halved spring onions, the whole lettuce and the whole skinned tomatoes, plenty of salt and pepper and whole herbs; close the lid and bake for a further half an hour.

## Tirit — BAKED BREAD WITH STEW

This is another country dish which makes use of old bread and left-over bits of meat and vegetables or cheese. The quantities are not very important.

*Thick slices of old bread (at least one slice per person)*
1 *lb lamb, mutton or veal*
1 *large onion*
3 *large tomatoes*
*A few sprigs parsley*
*A sprig thyme*
*Enough stock to cover the meat*

The old bread is baked in the oven until it is dry and crisp. Make a good stew with the lamb and vegetables and pour this over the crisp bread and serve with some yogurt.

Other sauces such as mince with white cheese, egg, cheese, chicken and yogurt can also be used.

## Kacamak — A FAMILY DISH FROM KASTAMONU

1 *measure of maize flour (polenta)*
2 *measures water*
1 *teaspoon salt*

Sauce:
1 *lb minced lamb or beef*
3 *medium tomatoes*
2 *green peppers*
2 *medium onions*
*Black pepper*
2 *ozs butter*

Put the measured water into a large pot and bring it to the boil and then add the maize flour to it with a teaspoon of salt and stir until it becomes a thick porridge; spread this porridge out on a large tray so that it is about half an inch thick and make depressions all over it with the back of a spoon.

Meanwhile make the sauce by frying the roughly sliced onions in the butter until they are soft and then adding the mince and roughly sliced tomatoes and peppers with plenty of seasoning. Simmer until they are all soft but not dry.

Pour this sauce over the porridge and bake in a hot oven for about fifteen minutes. Serve it hot with *ayran*.

**Çiğ Köfte** RAW RISSOLES

1 *lb lean minced lamb*
4 *ozs bulgur*
3 *long thin peppers (these are the hotter variety and will be about* 4 *or* 5 *ins long)*
1 *medium onion*
1 *teaspoon salt*

Put the *bulgur* into a basin and just cover it with hot water, which it will absorb in a little while; then knead it well into the mince.

Make a paste with the seeded peppers, onion and a teaspoon of salt by pounding them in a mortar. Add this paste to the mince and knead for twenty minutes and then put aside in a cool place to mature for three or four hours or overnight. Form this mixture into small balls which are eaten raw, the peppers rendering the meat digestible.

**İçli Köfte** STUFFED RISSOLES

1 *lb very lean minced lamb*
½ *lb bulgur*
*Salt*

For the stuffing:
1 *lb fatty lamb mince*
1 *medium onion*

*2 ozs butter* | *Paprika*
*Black pepper* | *A pinch salt*
*4 ozs rough ground walnuts*

Put the *bulgur* into a bowl and just cover with hot water. It will completely absorb the water in a little while, when it can be thoroughly mixed with the lean mince and a little salt and should then be kneaded for some time to get it really smooth. Form this mixture into little balls and leave aside.

Prepare the stuffing by frying the finely sliced onion in two ounces of butter until it is soft and then add the fatty mince. Keep stirring it until it is cooked through and dryish, then mix into it the walnuts, black pepper, paprika and a pinch of salt. Stir this all well together and then let it cool. Take a mince ball, make a hole in the middle and push in some of the stuffing and then close it up again rather as one would a Scotch egg. When all have been stuffed in this way, put them into a pot of boiling salty water and boil them gently for fifteen minutes. Test to see if they are done by carefully opening one with your fingers. When they are cooked lift them out with a drainer and serve with pickles and *ayran* or a salad.

**İzmir Köftesi** RISSOLES FROM IZMIR

*1 lb minced lamb*
*1 medium onion*
*1 egg*
*2 ozs finely chopped parsley*
*2 thick slices stale bread*
*½ teaspoon cummin*
*Salt and pepper*

Cut the edges off the bread and soak it in a little water and then crumble it into the mince together with the egg, grated onion, cummin, parsley, salt and pepper; knead this all very well with your hand and then form it into longish flat patties. Fry them in hot butter. Serve these köfte with a pilaf.

# *Meat and Chicken*

**Küzü Haşlama** LAMB WITH LEEKS

*2 lbs lamb from any cut*
*2 lbs leeks*
*½ a celery head or celeriac (optional)*
*4 large potatoes*
*5 sprigs parsley*
*Salt and pepper*

Cut the meat into serving-size pieces and brown them on both sides in a strong stew pot in the butter. Clean the leeks thoroughly but do not cut them up unless they are too large to lie flat in the pot; slice the celery lengthwise. Lay the leeks and the celery on top of the meat and above them the potatoes sliced in rings. Pour about two pints of water over the meat and season well and put in the sprigs of parsley. Simmer for two hours and then serve very hot in its own juice with some yogurt.

**Ciğerli Pilâv** LIVER WITH RICE

*1 lb liver*
*1 large onion*
*6 ozs rice*
*2 ozs butter*
*Stock*

Fry the roughly sliced onion in the butter and when it starts to get soft add the liver, which should be cut up into fairly small pieces about one inch square, and fry for a few minutes before adding the washed rice, seasoning and enough stock to come an inch above the level of the rice. Cook this as you would a pilaf and serve with yogurt.

**Kuzu Ciğer Dolması** TURKISH HAGGIS

*1 sheep's stomach membrane*
*1 lb sheep's liver*
*½ lb cooked rice*
*1 oz raisins*
*1 oz pine nuts*
*2 leaves of sage roughly chopped*
*3 medium tomatoes*
*3 ozs butter*
*Salt and pepper*

Fry the liver lightly in two ounces of butter and then chop it as small as possible and mix it with the rice, raisins, pine nuts, sage and seasoning, and stir for a little in the butter. Stuff this mixture into the sheep's stomach and sew it well closed with cotton; lay it in a baking dish with half an inch of water, the three skinned and sliced tomatoes and some salt and pepper and one ounce of butter. Bake it in a moderate oven (350) for thirty minutes. The top should be crisp and the bottom soft in the juice.

### Kokoreç — LAMB'S INTESTINES

This is an interesting dish which unexpectedly turned out to be rather good and is worth noting for anyone who might sample it in Turkey.

The intestines are wrapped around a horizontal spit and are grilled over a little portable charcoal fire which the vendor carries around in a long brass box rather like a shoe-cleaning boy. When you want to sample his ware, he puts the box down, cuts a slice off the hot grilled meat and sprinkles thyme and salt on it, places it between two thick slices of bread and hands it to you. I remember eating it in a crowded market with a little glass of tea and a slice of melon which the surrounding shopkeepers insisted on buying for me to go with *kokoreç*!

### Kadın Budu Köftesi — RICH RISSOLES

These *köfte* should be very smooth and round and soft like a woman's plump arms or thighs, from which it gets its name. 'Kadın' meaning woman and 'budu' meaning thigh.

| | |
|---|---|
| 1 *lb minced lamb* | 2 *eggs* |
| 1 *onion* | 1 *oz flour* |
| 4 *ozs cooked rice* | *Olive oil for frying* |
| 4 *ozs soft white cheese* | *Salt and black pepper* |

Mix the meat and grated onion together with the rice, cheese and one egg and season well. Knead very well indeed until you have a smooth mixture. Shape into balls about the size of a lemon, flatten very slightly, and dip into beaten egg and flour, and fry in very hot oil, turning until done.

## Işkembe

TRIPE

1 *sheep's tripe, about* 1 *lb*
½ *pint milk*
1 *large onion*
1 *oz flour*
1 *oz butter*
1 *lemon*
3 *or* 4 *cloves garlic*
3 *sprigs parsley*
*Salt and pepper*

Wash the tripe thoroughly and cover it with cold water and bring it to the boil quickly and then throw this water away. Return the tripe to the pot and cover with the milk, half a pint of water, the roughly sliced onions and some salt and simmer them for about two hours. Take the tripe out of the milk and cut it into thin strips and lay them on a dish. Make a roux with the butter and flour, add the tripe milk and then add to this the lemon juice, crushed garlic, finely chopped parsley, salt and pepper. Pour this sauce over the tripe and serve at once.

## Nohutlu Işkembe

TRIPE WITH CHICK PEAS

1 *sheep's tripe, about* 1 *lb*
1 *lemon*
3 *cloves garlic*
*Salt*
½ *lb chick peas*
4 *ozs butter*
2 *medium onions*
*Black pepper*

Soak the chick peas overnight, then put them into fresh water and boil them for about an hour until they are soft. Wash the tripe and put it in a pot, cover it with cold water and bring it quickly to the boil and then throw this water away. Cut the tripe into small pieces, cover with fresh water together with two strips of lemon rind, crushed garlic and salt, and simmer for two hours. When both the tripe and the chick peas are ready, fry the sliced onions in the butter until they are transparent and stir in the drained peas; add plenty of black pepper, salt and the tripe with about one pint of its broth. Simmer for a further twenty minutes. Serve the tripe hot, as it is, with a lemon sauce (page 133), or some paprika and chillies.

**Paça Haşlaması** STEWED SHEEP'S TROTTERS

*4 sheep's trotters*
*1 lemon*
*3 cloves garlic*
*A tablespoon olive oil*
*Salt*
*A tablespoon vinegar*
*A tablespoon finely chopped parsley*

Scrub the trotters clean under running water and then cover them with cold water and bring them to the boil; throw this water away and cover with fresh water together with the lemon rind, one clove of garlic, crushed, one tablespoonful of olive oil and salt. Simmer this for three or four hours, skimming if necessary. These trotters require long slow cooking and could be put in the slow oven of an Aga or Rayburn overnight. When they are sufficiently cooked, remove all the meat and put it on a serving dish with a little of the broth. Pour over them a sauce made with vinegar, the remaining two cloves of garlic, crushed, and parsley, simply mixed together or some yogurt with a little paprika sprinkled on it.

**Patlıcan Kebabı** LAMB WITH AUBERGINES

*1 lb lamb*
*3 round largish aubergines*
*2 medium onions*
*3 large tomatoes*
*2 ozs butter*
*1 teaspoon paprika*
*3 or 4 sprigs parsley*
*Salt and pepper*

Peel and cut the aubergines into slices, salt them well, place them between two plates and leave aside. Meanwhile cut the meat into small cubes and roughly slice the onions and skin the tomatoes. Heat one ounce of butter in a large pot and fry the onions and then add the meat and brown all over. When the meat is brown add the tomatoes, a teaspoon of paprika powder, parsley, salt and pepper, and simmer gently. Now rinse the aubergines and pat them dry and fry them in the rest of the butter in a separate pan until they are brown on both sides. Lay them carefully on top of the meat; pour in half a pint of water and simmer them all very gently for one hour. Do not stir the pot but shake it occasionally, as the aubergines should not be mixed into the meat but remain intact on top. Serve it with a pilaf or with yogurt.

**Domatesli Köfte** RISSOLES WITH TOMATOES

*1 lb minced lamb or beef*
*2 thick slices oldish bread*
*Wine or water*
*2 medium onions*
*1 egg*
*6 large tomatoes*
*2 cloves garlic*
*3 or 4 sprigs parsley for cooking with extra for garnishing*
*A good pinch dry basil*
*1 bay leaf*
*1 tablespoon olive oil*
*Salt and pepper*

Cut the edges off the bread and soak it in a little water or wine. Then squeeze it out in your hand and crumble it into the mince, together with one grated onion, the egg, finely chopped parsley and plenty of salt and pepper. Knead the meat thoroughly and when it is smooth form it into little balls the size of a small egg. Heat one tablespoonful of olive oil and fry the meat balls until they are brown all over. Meanwhile cook the skinned and roughly chopped tomatoes in a large pot with the finely sliced second onion, crushed garlic, basil, bay leaf and salt and pepper to taste. Simmer for a few minutes and then drop in the meat balls and cook both together for a further twenty minutes. Serve with plenty of roughly chopped parsley on top.

**Bahcıvan Kebabı** COUNTRY STEW

*2 lbs mutton or lamb*
*3 medium carrots*
*3 large tomatoes*
*1 green capsicum*
*½ lb fresh peas*
*20 shallots or 3 large onions*
*2 cloves garlic*
*3 sprigs parsley*
*2 pints stock*
*2 ozs butter*

Cut the meat into small cubes and brown them in the butter in a strong deep pot; add the diced carrots. Lower the heat and cook until the carrots begin to soften, shaking the pot from time to time. Now add the skinned tomatoes, sliced pepper, peas and sliced onions; season well and put in the crushed garlic, the stock and the sprigs of parsley, and simmer for one hour. Serve with a bowl of yogurt and paprika.

**Kekikli Bonfile** FILLET OF BEEF WITH THYME

*1 lb fillet of beef in a whole piece*
*¼ pint white wine*
*3 cloves garlic*
*3 large tomatoes*
*1 oz chopped thyme*
*1 oz butter*
*Salt and pepper*

Rub the meat all over with salt and two cloves of the garlic, crushed, and place it in a roasting tin with the butter; roast it in a hot oven (400) for fifteen minutes on each side and then pour the wine over the meat and cook for a further ten minutes.

Make a tomato purée with the skinned tomatoes, the butter and the thyme, one clove of garlic, salt and pepper.

Place the fillet on a warm serving dish. Mix all the remaining juices from the meat into the purée and pour it over the meat. Serve at once with fried potatoes and a salad.

**Beyin Haşlaması** COLD BRAINS

*3 sheep's brains (or 1 lb)*
*1 large onion*
*1 tablespoon vinegar*
*3 or 4 sprigs parsley*

*Juice of 1 lemon*
*1 tablespoon olive oil*
*Salt and pepper*
*Black pepper*

Clean the brains under running water and remove the membrane by pulling it off the meat. Cover them with cold water, bring to the boil quickly and throw this water away. Now put them into fresh water with the roughly sliced onion, vinegar and seasoning, and simmer them for twenty minutes. Allow them to cool and then cut them into small pieces.

Make a lemon sauce with the juice from the lemon and a tablespoon of olive oil and the finely chopped parsley. Mix the brains well in this and arrange on a serving dish. Serve cold, sprinkled with black pepper.

**Beyin Tavası** FRIED BRAINS

*2 sheep's brains, about ¾ lb*
*1 egg*
*1 oz flour*
*2 tablespoons olive oil*
*Salt and pepper*

Wash the brains well in cold water and remove the membrane. Bring them to the boil quickly in salty water and simmer for about five minutes. Drain and cool and cut into pieces. Dip the pieces into beaten egg and seasoned flour and fry in hot oil until golden. Serve with a lemon and parsley sauce (see page 134).

**İstanbul Köftesi** *or* **Terbiyeli Köfte** RISSOLES IN BROTH

*1 lb minced lamb or beef*
*1 medium onion*
*2 tablespoons cooked rice*
*A little cornstarch flour*
*2 eggs*
*2 pints meat stock*
*Juice of 1 lemon*
*4 or 5 sprigs parsley*
*Salt and pepper*

This dish is a bit soupy, but you can reduce the amount of liquid when it is being served.

Grate the onion into the mince and mix with the rice, parsley and one egg. Season well and knead into a smooth texture. Form into little balls about the size of a walnut and roll in the cornstarch.

Have the stock (it can be made with a meat cube) boiling gently and drop the balls into it and boil for fifteen minutes. Beat the other egg and add the lemon juice slowly and a little of the stock. When the meat balls are cooked, draw the pot off the heat and add the lemon sauce to it. Serve immediately with finely chopped parsley sprinkled on top.

**Kuzu Kapama** LAMB BAKED WITH VEGETABLES

2 *lbs lamb taken from any cut (neck, shoulder or leg)*
2 *medium aubergines*
6 *large tomatoes*
6 *medium potatoes*
4 *large leeks*
2 *courgettes*
2 *green peppers*
4 *cloves garlic*
*A few sprigs rosemary*
*A good pinch basil*
5 *sprigs parsley*
2 *tablespoons olive oil*
*Salt and pepper*

The meat should be cut into chop-size pieces, not too small. Slice the aubergines and salt well, place them between two plates and leave aside for twenty minutes. Rub the meat well with some crushed garlic and salt, and fry it until brown on both sides in the olive oil. Transfer the meat to a large roasting pan and spread it out in the bottom. Slice all the other vegetables quite thinly and put them in layers on top of the meat. Rinse the aubergines well and add them, finishing up with a layer of potatoes. Season well and add the herbs, little slices of garlic dotted around, and one cup of water. Bake in a hot oven (400) for one and a half hours until everything is well cooked. Serve as it is with plenty of bread.

**Kuzu Kızartmasi** LAMB SHANKS COOKED WITH PAPRIKA

*4 to 6 lamb shanks*
*4 medium potatoes*
*5 large tomatoes*
*1 teaspoon paprika*
*Salt to taste*
*Garlic*
*A few sprigs rosemary*

Rub the shanks well with a generous amount of paprika powder and crushed garlic with salt. Put them in a roasting pan, cover with the skinned tomatoes and the potatoes sliced into rings and season well. Add about half a pint of water and some rosemary, and bake in a moderate oven (350) for two hours.

**Cızbız Köfte** SIZZLING RISSOLES

*1 lb minced lamb*
*3 thick slices oldish bread*
*1 medium onion*
*1 egg*
*3 or 4 sprigs parsley*
*2 tablespoons wine (optional)*
*Olive oil*
*Salt and black pepper*

Cut the edges off the bread and soak it in one tablespoon of water and two tablespoonfuls of wine; squeeze it out and crumble it into the mince together with the grated onion, roughly chopped parsley, egg and seasoning. Knead until you have a very smooth mixture with no lumps at all. Divide it into egg-size balls and roll these into slightly flattened sausages. Brush them with olive oil and grill under a very hot fire until brown on both sides. They can also be threaded longwise on *şiş* sticks and grilled in the same way. They can be eaten with pilaf or on bread with a yogurt sauce poured over them and they are especially good with the hot capsicum peppers, which are so popular in Turkey.

**Tavuk Fırın** ROAST CHICKEN

*1 chicken*
*2 tablespoons olive oil*
*1 teaspoon salt*
*1 teaspoon paprika*

Rub the chicken all over with salt and plenty of paprika powder so that it is quite red and pour over it a generous amount of olive oil and rub that in too; this will give the chicken a delicious, crisp skin. Roast the chicken in a hot oven (400) for about an hour and put it on a serving dish; pour off all the oil and make a gravy with the remaining juices and a little stock made from the giblets. Serve the chicken with a pilaf.

**Çerkes Tavuğu** CIRCASSIAN CHICKEN

- 1 *chicken*
- 2 *medium thick slices oldish bread*
- 2 *cloves garlic*
- 8 *ozs walnuts*
- 1 *medium onion*
- 1 *teaspoon paprika*
- *A few leaves tarragon*
- *A few sprigs parsley*
- *Salt and pepper*

Cover the chicken with cold water to which has been added the onion, tarragon, parsley and seasoning, and simmer for one hour until the chicken is tender but not over-cooked. Allow it to cool a little and then take off all the flesh and shred it into very fine slices with a sharp knife.

Meanwhile put the walnuts through a fine mixer *three times*, saving all the oil which comes out. Soak the bread in a little of the chicken stock and then crumble it into a pan with the crushed garlic, salt and pepper. Mix them well together and stir them over a gentle heat: add the walnuts and a cup of chicken broth and stir until you have a smooth thick sauce.

Arrange the chicken in a serving dish and pour the sauce over it and stir well in. Mix the paprika with the walnut oil and pour this over the chicken as well. This dish is always served a little cooled.

NOTE This famous dish had many regional variations. One such dish is to bind the chicken and walnut sauce with a beaten egg and form little cutlets which are dipped in egg and breadcrumbs and fried until golden.

**Beyaz Soslu Tavuk** CHICKEN IN A WHITE SAUCE

*1 medium chicken*
*2 eggs*
*1 tablespoon flour*
*2 cloves garlic*
*Juice of 1 lemon*
*Teaspoon vinegar*
*3 or 4 sprigs parsley*
*Salt and pepper*
*4 slices bread*

Simmer the chicken in plenty of water to which has been added the onion, parsley and seasoning, for one hour.

Make the sauce by beating the eggs in a double saucepan and adding the flour, lemon juice, vinegar and the crushed garlic and seasoning and stirring until it is smooth; thin it with a little of the chicken broth.

Toast four slices of bread, lay them in a warm serving dish and pour a little of the broth over them. Take all the meat off the chicken and lay it over the bread and pour the sauce over them all. Sprinkle with the finely chopped parsley and serve at once.

**Piliç Güveci Sebzeli** CHICKEN WITH VEGETABLES

*1 chicken*
*2 medium onions*
*2 aubergines*
*1 lb green beans*
*2 courgettes*
*3 large tomatoes*
*2 green peppers*
*¼ lb or 1 small tin of okra*
*3 tablespoons olive oil*

Peel and slice the aubergines in rings and cover them with salt and leave them aside between two plates for twenty minutes. Finely slice the onions, string the beans, peel and slice the courgettes, skin the tomatoes, seed the peppers and slice the okra.

Joint the chicken. Roll the pieces in seasoned flour and fry them in the olive oil until they start to brown and then lay them aside. In the same oil fry the rinsed and dried aubergines and then the rest of the vegetables for a few minutes. Place all the vegetables except the tomatoes in the bottom of a casserole, and lay the chicken on top of them and then the sliced tomatoes; season well and add half a pint of water. Cover the casserole and bake for an hour in a moderate oven (350).

**Piliç Yahnisi** CHICKEN CASSEROLE

1 *chicken*
2 *medium onions*
1 *celery head or celeriac*
4 *ozs mushrooms*
3 *large tomatoes*
3 *cloves garlic*
1 *oz flour*
1 *sprig rosemary*
3 *or* 4 *sprigs parsley*
3 *tablespoons olive oil*
*Salt and pepper*

Cut the chicken into serving-size pieces and roll them in seasoned flour. Heat the olive oil in a frying pan and fry the pieces of chicken quickly all over until they are slightly browned and then transfer them to a casserole dish. Fry the thinly sliced onions and the celery and the whole mushrooms in the same oil for a few minutes and then lay them on top of the chicken, together with the sliced skinned tomatoes, garlic herbs and seasoning; cover the casserole with a wineglass of water and close the lid. Bake in a moderate oven (350) for one hour. It is very important not to over-cook chickens in casseroles as this will render them dull and tasteless.

**Piliç Tencerede** BRAISED CHICKEN

1 *medium chicken*
3 *medium onions*
2 *small carrots*
4 *large tomatoes*
2 *cloves garlic*
*A few leaves tarragon*
*A few sprigs parsley*
2 *tablespoons olive oil*
*Salt and pepper*

In a large strong pot heat the olive oil and fry the whole

chicken all over until it starts to brown a little; then add the thickly sliced onions and the scraped carrots and fry a little more; finally put in the tomatoes, garlic, herbs and seasoning with enough water to come half-way up the bird and simmer all gently for about an hour. Serve with a little of the broth around it.

## Piliç Izgara — GRILLED CHICKEN

It is a common sight in Turkey to see whole chickens slowly turning on a spit over a charcoal fire. For home use I find it easier to joint the chicken or split open a young spring chicken and then grill it quickly on each side. It will be even tastier if the chicken is allowed to marinate in a mixture of olive oil, a few cloves of crushed garlic, the juice of a lemon and some seasoning. The object of grilling is to cook through the meat as quickly as possible without rendering it hard and dry: this needs careful watching but the results are rewarding.

A hot grilled chicken is delicious with a salad or a pilaf and is often a popular picnic dish on family outings, eaten under the trees by some water, where Turkish families love to spend their weekends.

## Keşkek — A TRADITIONAL DISH OF CHICKEN AND WHEAT

1 *chicken of average size*
½ *lb bulgur*
1 *quart water*
1 *oz butter*
1 *teaspoon paprika*
½ *teaspoon salt*
*Black pepper to taste*

Put the *bulgur* into a large basin and cover it with cold water to a level just above the grains and leave it to soak overnight by which time the wheat will have soaked up all the water. Simmer the chicken in a quart of water, well seasoned with salt and pepper, until it is tender (about one hour) and allow it to cool in the broth. Then take all the meat off the chicken, shred it as finely as you can with a sharp knife and return it to the broth. Now add the wet wheat and salt and pepper to the chicken and simmer them together, stirring and beating continuously until the mixture resembles a thick porridge. This may take at least twenty minutes. Serve it hot in little bowls and sprinkled over with a little melted butter into which has been stirred a teaspoon of paprika.

**Tavuk Köftesi** CHICKEN RISSOLES

- ¾ *lb cold cooked chicken or turkey*
- 2 *ozs butter*
- 2 *ozs flour*
- 2 *ozs white cheese*
- 1 *egg*
- 2 *sprigs parsley*
- *A pinch of thyme*
- *Olive oil for frying*
- *Salt and pepper*

Mince the cold chicken quite fine and season with a little salt and pepper, thyme and finely chopped parsley. Make a *very stiff* roux with the butter and flour, add the cheese and a very little milk and then beat in the egg and allow it to cool a little. Now mix in the chicken and beat it until you have a dough that can be shaped into little balls about the size of a small egg. Fry the balls in shallow hot oil until they are golden all over.

# *Vegetable Dishes*

As I have said at the beginning of the 'Meat' section, the Turkish practice is to include under the general heading of 'Vegetables' many dishes which also contain a fair proportion of meat.

Individual vegetables are seldom cooked entirely on their own, but usually form the mainstay of a dish which becomes a course by itself: these vegetable stews are extremely useful and economical and can be adapted in many different ways to suit available vegetables. The Turks like their vegetables well cooked and served in plenty of juice. There are many cold dishes made with olive oil which are very refreshing in the summer, *Imam bayıldı* being perhaps the best known. Artichokes and aubergines are great favourites and there are so many ways of cooking aubergines that one never tires of them.

The variety and abundance of vegetables which confront one in the markets is quite bewildering and one can hardly make up one's mind which to buy. Aubergines are long or square, varying from light mauve to deep purple. The tomatoes are large and ribbed and have a strong flavour; where one or two would do in Turkey, three or four must be substituted in countries where the tomato is a much more puny specimen. Tomatoes are greatly used in Turkish cooking and there is hardly a meal when they are not present in some form or other. Courgettes, cucumbers and marrows abound in every shape, although the portly vegetable marrow is never allowed to develop. There is an astonishing variety of string beans ranging from green to red, pink and white. They are not to be confused with the dry bean family such as green or red lentils, split peas, kidney and haricot beans which also present a wide choice. Peppers, or capsicums, as they are called, are both red and green, square and long, some the size of a finger and some the size of a turnip. They vary in hotness, which can be gauged from the strength of the smell of their seeds: if the smell is strong they will be very hot, whereas others can be quite mild.

When preparing aubergines, they should always be salted heavily after cutting or slicing, and placed between two plates and left for about twenty minutes so that the bitter juices can be drawn out. They are then rinsed well and dried in a cloth before cooking.

Peppers should be seeded and the inner pulp removed. Tomatoes are usually skinned, which can be easily done by immersing them in boiling water for a minute and then peeling off the loosened skin.

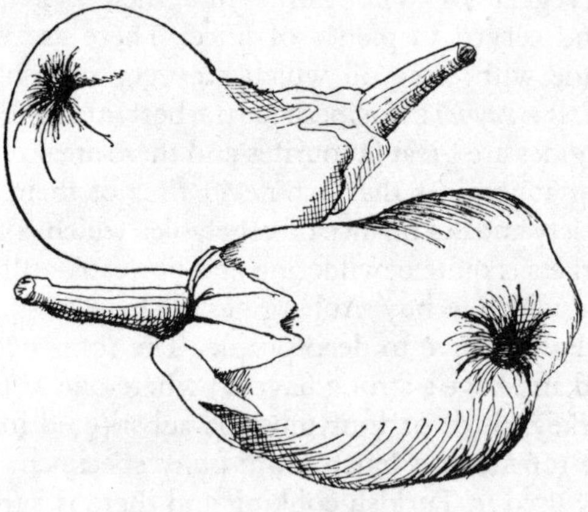

Garlic is used quite a lot, especially in the cold oil dishes, and although the amount can be varied, they would not be typical if the garlic was omitted altogether. Garlic should be skinned which is most easily done by banging it once or twice with the back of a heavy kitchen knife so that the skin falls off. It should then be crushed with a little salt, which helps to bring out the juice and flavour, before using.

Olive oil, being plentiful in Turkey and cheaper than it is in Britain, is used in quantity, and one can always reduce the amount a bit. Hot dishes are usually cooked in butter or margarine, but olive oil is always used for cold dishes as it does not congeal.

Yogurt is often served with vegetables and goes very well with them.

**Enginar Zeytinyağlı** ARTICHOKES IN OIL

1 *artichoke per person*
10 *spring onions*
*Juice of 2 lemons*
¼ *pint olive oil*
½ *oz flour*
1 *medium carrot*
1 *tablespoon sugar*
*A few sprigs of dill and parsley*
*Salt and pepper*

Boil the artichokes just as they are in plain water for about fifteen minutes until they are tender enough to handle. Then hold them by the stalk and carefully remove the outer leaves so that you are left with the inside and base. Take out the inner flowers and place the artichokes immediately into a basin containing the juice of one lemon and the flour and enough water to cover them; this will preserve their colour. When they are all prepared place them in a clean deep pot with their stalks standing up. Pour over them the olive oil, sugar, seasoning, diced carrot, spring onions and the juice of the other lemon, and use some of the water in which you boiled them to just cover their bases. Close the pot and simmer for about an hour. Allow them to cool in the pot. Remove them to a serving dish and pour over them the juice in which they have been cooked and sprinkle with roughly chopped dill and parsley. Serve very cold.

**Etli Kereviz** CELERY WITH LAMB

*1 lb shoulder or leg of lamb*
*1 large onion*
*1 good-sized celery head or celeriac*
*2 eggs*
*2 ozs butter*
*Juice of 1 lemon*
*3 cups water*
*Salt and pepper*

Cut the meat into pieces each about the size of a large chop and brown them well in the butter in a deep pot. Slice the onion and celery into rings and add to the meat together with the water and some seasoning, and simmer gently for forty-five minutes. Beat the eggs and gradually add the lemon juice to them, beating all the time. Take some of the stock from the pot and add it slowly to the eggs until the sauce becomes smooth. Pour it over the meat and stir it in a bit, but do *not* allow the broth to boil again. Heat very carefully before serving.

**Pirinçli Domates** TOMATOES WITH RICE ON TOP

*6 large tomatoes*
*A few tablespoons of washed rice*
*A pinch of dry chervil*
*A pinch of dry basil*
*Salt and pepper*

Wipe the tomatoes, cut them in half and sprinkle them lightly with salt and arrange them on a baking tray with the cut side facing upwards. Carefully spoon on enough rice to cover the top of each tomato, without spilling any into the tray. Add enough water to come almost up to the level of the rice without actually touching it. Sprinkle the herbs and seasoning over them and bake them in a moderate oven (350) until the rice has absorbed the water and the tomatoes are cooked through. Serve as it is in the dish.

**Kabak Müjveri** MARROW RISSOLES

This recipe uses only the inside of the marrow which is often thrown away when the marrows are stuffed. In this way two dishes can be made from the same marrow.

| | |
|---|---|
| *Insides of one large or several small marrows* | 2 *ozs cream cheese* |
| 1 *lb minced lamb* | 1 *oz flour* |
| 2 *eggs* | *A few sprigs dill or chervil* |
| 1 *large grated onion* | 2 *tablespoons olive oil* |
| | *Salt and pepper* |

Seed the marrow flesh and put it into a bowl together with the other ingredients and knead them all well together. Use just enough flour to give a bit of firmness and season well. Shape into rissoles and fry in hot oil.

**Prasa Yahnisi** STEWED LEEKS

| | |
|---|---|
| 2 *lbs leeks* | ¼ *pint olive oil* |
| 2 *large onions* | ½ *pint stock* |
| 1 *large tomato* | *A few sprigs dill* |

Take off any coarse outer leaves and wash the leeks in plenty of running water to remove all the grit. Cut them into half lengths. Slice the onions into rings and fry them in the oil until they are soft and then add the leeks; turn them over several times in the oil, then add the skinned tomato and seasoning, and cover with some stock. Simmer gently for half an hour. Serve either hot or cold with chopped dill.

**Patlıcan Kebabı** AUBERGINE PURÉE

| | |
|---|---|
| 2 *large round aubergines make enough for four people* | 2 *tablespoons yogurt* |
| 1 *tablespoon olive oil* | *Juice of* 1 *lemon* |
| | 2 *cloves garlic* |

*1 oz cream cheese*
*Black olives and parsley for garnishing*
*Salt*

Wipe the aubergines and place them directly on to the hot plate of the stove and keep turning them over until the skin is brown and the insides feel very soft. Take care not to break the skin during this process. Hold them in a cloth and slit open one side and scoop out all the pulp into a bowl and add the lemon juice immediately to prevent discoloration. Now mix in gradually the olive oil, crushed garlic, some salt, yogurt and cream cheese and beat them vigorously until you have a very smooth purée. A few seconds in an electric mixer gives it a very light colour and is a great improvement, but the Turkish cook would expect to rely on her elbow grease. Spread out on a flat serving dish and garnish with black olives and parsley. Chill well before serving.

The method of cooking the aubergines on top of the stove gives them a slightly smoky taste which is most characteristic of the dish. It is important that the aubergine is well cooked inside before mixing it into a purée or it will have rather a bitter taste. If it seems insufficiently soft after scooping it out, it should be simmered in a pan for a little before using.

**Kapuska** CABBAGE

*1 cabbage*
*1 large onion*
*2 large tomatoes*
*1 oz butter*

Grate the onion and skin and chop the tomatoes and simmer them together in a deep pot in the butter. Wash and slice the cabbage finely and add to the pot, season and cook slowly for half an hour. There should be enough water on the cabbage after washing without adding any more and this method will give it a better flavour.

## Hünkâr Beğendi

AUBERGINE PURÉE WITH LAMB

- 2 *large round aubergines*
- 1 *lb lamb from the leg*
- 1 *large onion*
- 2 *tablespoons tomato purée*
- 1 *tablespoon butter*
- 1 *cup water*
- 1 *oz flour*
- 1 *oz margarine*
- ¼ *pint milk*
- 2 *ozs grated white cheese*
- *Juice of* 1 *lemon*
- *A few sprigs parsley*
- *Salt and pepper*

Cut the meat into small cubes about one inch square and finely slice the onion. Brown them both in the butter and then add the tomato purée, sprigs of parsley, seasoning and water and simmer very gently for one hour.

Meanwhile make the aubergine purée. Lay the aubergines directly on to the hot plate or just above the gas and keep turning them over and over until the skin begins to brown and they become soft inside. Be careful not to break the skin and continue turning until you have something resembling a baked potato. When all the inside feels soft it is ready. This method is much quicker than baking and is more typically Turkish. Now hold the aubergines in a cloth and cut down one side and scoop out the pulp into a bowl and add the lemon juice immediately to prevent discoloration. Beat the aubergines well into the lemon juice until they are quite light. Now make a roux with the margarine and flour and add the milk and grated cheese and beat all this into the aubergines until you have something resembling English mashed potatoes. Put this into the centre of a large serving dish and smooth it out and then pour the lamb stew over it. Sprinkle with finely chopped parsley and serve hot.

## Pirinçli İspanak

SPINACH WITH RICE

- 2 *lbs spinach*
- 1 *large onion*
- 4 *ozs rice*
- ¼ *pint tomato purée*
- 2 *ozs margarine*
- *Salt and pepper*

Wash the spinach thoroughly, drain it and then chop it up fairly well. Wash the rice until the water runs clear and drain in a sieve. Slice the onion very finely, fry it lightly in the margarine in the bottom of a deep pot then lay the spinach on top of the onion and the rice on top of the spinach; pour the tomato purée over them and season well. Cover the pot and cook gently until the rice is soft and all the liquid has been absorbed. Do not stir this dish as it will spoil the appearance but shake it from time to time if necessary. Tip out on to a warm dish carefully.

**Patlıcan Tavası** FRIED AUBERGINE

- 2 *or* 3 *long aubergines*
- 2 *medium tomatoes*
- 2 *cloves garlic*
- 3 *tablespoons olive oil*
- 1 *large green pepper*
- ½ *pint yogurt*
- *Salt*

Wash the aubergines, peel and slice them into rounds; cover them with salt and place between two plates and leave them to draw for twenty minutes. Skin and cut up the tomatoes, seed and slice the pepper. Beat the yogurt with the crushed garlic and a little salt and water. Heat about three tablespoons of olive oil and allow it to become very hot. Rinse and pat dry the aubergines and then fry them in the oil until they are brown on both sides and drain them on absorbent paper and keep warm. Now fry the tomatoes and peppers in the same oil for a few minutes and add them to the aubergines and serve immediately with the yogurt poured over them.

NOTE Aubergines, after slicing and salting, can also be floured and dipped quickly into some beer, and then fried. This gives a delicious flavour to the aubergines and was suggested to me by an excellent Turkish cook in Ankara.

## **İmam Bayıldı** AUBERGINES WITH OIL AND GARLIC

The name of this dish means 'The Fainting Imam'. No one is quite sure whether he was supposed to have fainted at the extreme richness of the dish or at the extravagance of his wife in all the olive oil she used in preparing it! If he did feel that his purse had been over-taxed, I am sure he soon forgave her when he tasted this sumptuous arrangement.

| | |
|---|---|
| 6 *long aubergines* | *Juice of* 1 *lemon* |
| 3 *large onions* | *A few sprigs parsley* |
| 6 *large tomatoes for the stuffing, with some extra for slicing* | 1 *teaspoon sugar* |
| 6 *to* 10 *cloves garlic (this dish depends on a lot of garlic if it is to be characteristic)* | ½ *pint olive oil* |
| | ½ *pint mild stock* |
| | *Salt and pepper* |

The long type of aubergine is best used for this dish; wash them and then make a deep slit from end to end without actually breaking open the ends and then push the ends gently towards the middle in order to open the slit. Salt the insides well and leave for fifteen minutes.

Meanwhile slice the onions very finely and fry them in a tablespoon of olive oil until they are soft. Put them into a bowl and mix into them the skinned and chopped tomatoes, the crushed garlic, roughly chopped parsley and seasoning and stir them well together.

Rinse out the aubergines and pat them dry. Heat some more oil and fry the aubergines very carefully, all over, taking care not to spoil their shape. Arrange them in a baking dish and fill the slits with the tomato mixture and cover each one with some slices of skinned tomatoes. Pour over them all the remaining oil, as well as the oil from the frying, and enough stock to come half-way up the sides of the aubergines, as well as the juice of a lemon, the sugar, and some salt. Bake them in a moderate oven (350) for about an hour and then leave to cool.

This dish is always eaten cold and makes an excellent start to a meal. If you find it too oily, reduce the amount you use

**Patlıcan Karnıyarık** LONG STUFFED AUBERGINES

Choose long plump aubergines for this dish and leave the stalks on. They look rather like little boats with a cargo of meat when they are served. They are very popular and make an excellent light meal with some yogurt and a salad.

| | |
|---|---|
| 1 *long aubergine for each person* | ½ *pint stock* |
| 2 *medium onions* | 3 *ozs margarine* |
| 1 *lb minced lamb* | *A few sprigs parsley* |
| 3 *large tomatoes* | |

Wash the aubergines and make a deep slit from end to end without actually breaking open the ends. Press open and sprinkle liberally with salt and leave aside.

Meanwhile chop up the onions finely and brown them in one ounce of margarine; add the mince, fry a little more and then add two of the tomatoes, skinned and chopped, and parsley and season well. Simmer until most of the juice has cooked away.

Rinse out the aubergines and pat dry. Heat a further two ounces of margarine, and fry the aubergines all over carefully so that you do not spoil their shape. Arrange them on a large baking dish and stuff each one carefully with the mixture. Cover them with slices of tomato and pour around them enough stock to come half-way up their sides. Bake in a moderate oven (350) for about forty-five minutes until they are soft and well cooked through. Serve as they are in their juice.

**Taze Fasulye Etli** GREEN BEANS WITH LAMB

| | |
|---|---|
| 1 *lb lamb taken from the leg* | 1 *lb green beans* |
| 1 *large onion* | 3 *large tomatoes* |

*3 cloves garlic*
*3 ozs butter*
*1½ pints water*
*Salt and pepper*

Bone the meat and cut it up into small cubes about one inch square. Slice the onions into thin rings and fry them in the butter until they just begin to turn golden, then add the meat and fry it until it begins to brown a little, then add the skinned tomatoes, crushed garlic and seasoning. String the beans and break them in half and then add them to the meat together with the water. Simmer gently for about one hour until the beans are well cooked and quite soft. Serve as it is in its own juice.

### Taze Fasulye Zeytinyağlı — GREEN BEANS IN OIL

*1 lb green beans*
*3 tablespoons olive oil*
*2 medium onions*
*3 large tomatoes*
*3 cloves garlic*
*1 teaspoon sugar*
*Juice of 1 lemon*
*½ teaspoon salt*
*Pepper to taste*

Wash and string the beans and break them into halves. Slice the onions finely and fry them in the olive oil until they become transparent and then add the skinned tomatoes and continue to cook until they start to get soft. Stir in the beans and turn them well over in the oil before adding the crushed garlic, sugar, salt and just enough water to cover them. Simmer the beans for one hour and then leave them to cool in the pot. Just before serving them (cold) squeeze the lemon juice over them. If you want to eat this dish hot, which is also very good, cook it with two ounces of butter instead of the oil.

### Sebze Bastısı — VEGETABLE STEW

*2 long aubergines*
*4 medium tomatoes*
*2 green peppers*
*2 medium courgettes*
*½ lb French beans*
*3 cloves garlic*

*2 ozs butter*
*A few sprigs dill and parsley*
*Mild stock as needed*
*Salt and pepper*

Slice the aubergines into quarter-inch thick rings and put them between two plates with plenty of salt on them and leave to draw for twenty minutes. Meanwhile skin the tomatoes, seed the peppers, peel the courgettes, and string the beans if necessary; cut them all up into thick slices except the beans which should be broken. Rinse the aubergines thoroughly, pat them dry and then fry them in the butter on both sides. Transfer them to a baking dish. Fry the rest of the vegetables in the same butter and place them on top of the aubergines. Add the crushed garlic, herbs, seasoning and enough stock to come half-way up the vegetables and bake in a moderate oven (350) for one hour or until they are done. Serve in their dish with some yogurt.

**Barbunya Fasulye Zeytinyağlı** RED BEANS IN OIL

½ *lb red or kidney beans*
1 *large onion*
2 *medium tomatoes*
3 *cloves garlic*
2 *tablespoons olive oil*
½ *pint bean stock*
*A few sprigs parsley*
*Pinch of dry chervil*
*Salt and pepper*

Soak the beans overnight and then boil them in plenty of salty water until they are soft, but not broken. Meanwhile fry the finely sliced onion in the oil and add the skinned, roughly chopped tomatoes, crushed garlic and seasoning. Add the drained beans to this with half a pint of the bean stock and simmer for a further ten minutes. Pour into a dish and serve cold with roughly chopped parsley and chervil on top.

**Mercimek Köftesi** LENTIL CAKES

2 *ozs lentils*
4 *ozs bulgur*
1 *large onion*
1 *teaspoon cummin*

| | |
|---|---|
| *1 teaspoon paprika* | *1 pint water* |
| *1 oz butter* | *Salt* |
| *A few sprigs parsley* | |

Wash the lentils and rinse until clean. Put them in a pot and add one pint of water and a little salt. Boil the lentils until they are soft; this will not use up all the water. Now add the *bulgur* to the lentils and water and allow them to soak for about an hour. All the water should then be absorbed by the wheat and you will have a moist type of dough. Meanwhile fry the finely sliced onion in one ounce of butter until it becomes transparent and then stir in the cummin and paprika and finely chopped parsley. Now put the lentil dough in a bowl and thoroughly mix into it the onion and spices. Knead them together for two or three minutes, then form into little cakes about two inches in diameter and arrange them on a dish. They are eaten without further cooking and are served with hot peppers or salad.

**Domatesli Fasulye** HARICOT BEANS WITH TOMATOES

| | |
|---|---|
| *½ lb haricot beans* | *1 oz butter* |
| *4 large tomatoes* | *A pinch dry basil* |
| *1 large onion* | *3 sprigs parsley* |
| *2 or 3 cloves garlic* | *Salt and pepper* |

Soak the beans overnight and then simmer them in fresh water, to which a pinch of salt has been added, until they are soft. Prepare a tomato purée by frying the finely sliced onion in the butter until it becomes transparent and then adding the skinned and chopped tomatoes, crushed garlic, basil, finely chopped parsley and seasoning. Allow them to simmer for five minutes. Strain the beans into a serving dish and pour the tomato purée over them and stir it well in, adding a little of the bean water if it seems too dry. The beans can be eaten hot or cold.

This is a very common dish and is often eaten hot for breakfast.

**Havuc Kızartması** FRIED CARROTS

| | |
|---|---|
| 1 *lb carrots* | ½ *pint yogurt* |
| ½ *oz flour* | ½ *teaspoon caraway seeds* |
| 2 *tablespoons olive oil* | *Salt and pepper* |

Peel and slice the carrots into quarter-inch rings and parboil them in salty water. When they are almost soft, drain them and cool a little. Toss them in the seasoned flour and then fry them in the hot oil until they are brown. Arrange them in a serving dish and pour over them the warmed yogurt and sprinkle with the caraway seeds.

**Patates Kıymalı** POTATOES WITH MINCE

| | |
|---|---|
| 1 *lb potatoes* | 2 *or* 3 *cloves garlic* |
| 1 *lb minced lamb* | ½ *pint mild stock* |
| 2 *large onions* | 3 *sprigs parsley* |
| 3 *large tomatoes* | *A pinch basil* |
| 2 *teaspoons paprika powder* | 2 *ozs butter* |

Fry the roughly sliced onions in the butter and when they begin to soften add the skinned and roughly chopped tomatoes, mince, crushed garlic, paprika and herbs. Allow this to simmer for about five minutes. Peel the potatoes and slice them into quarter-inch thick rings and fry them in hot oil until they are brown on both sides. Now pour the meat mixture into a deep oven dish, lay the potatoes on top and carefully pour in the stock and seasoning. Put into a moderate oven (350) for about an hour. Serve with a bowl of yogurt.

**Domatesli Patates** POTATOES WITH TOMATOES

| | |
|---|---|
| 1 *lb potatoes* | ½ *pint mild stock* |
| 2 *large onions* | 3 *sprigs parsley* |
| 4 *large tomatoes* | *A pinch chervil* |
| 3 *cloves garlic* | *Salt and pepper* |
| 1 *oz butter* | |

Peel and slice the potatoes into rings about the thickness of two pennies. Slice the onions into thin rings without breaking them. Lay them carefully in the hot butter and fry until they are transparent; then transfer them to a baking dish. Now lay the potato rings on top of the onions and then lay the skinned and sliced tomatoes in a layer over the potatoes. Season well and add the crushed garlic, finely chopped parsley and the stock. Bake in a hot oven (400) until the potatoes are cooked through and then serve with a little chervil sprinkled over the top.

**Etli Dolma** MEAT STUFFING FOR HOT DOLMAS

This stuffing is used for tomatoes, peppers, aubergines and courgettes and is served as a *hot* vegetable dish.

| | |
|---|---|
| 1 *lb minced lamb or beef* | ½ *cup rice* |
| 2 *medium onions* | ½ *cup water* |

*1 oz butter*
*A few sprigs dill*
*A few sprigs parsley*
*Salt and pepper*

Choose large square-shaped vegetables for stuffing as these will stand up better and hold more. Cut off the tops and keep them for lids; scoop out the insides and sprinkle with salt. (Aubergines should be heavily salted and then rinsed out in twenty minutes time.)

To make the stuffing, melt the butter in a pan and put in the washed rice, fry it for a few minutes and then cover it with water or stock to come just over the top of the rice. Boil out the water quite fast so that the grains are fairly dry and allow it to cool. Put the mince into a bowl, grate the onions into it and add some of the chopped parsley. Mix the rice into the meat and knead them all together until you have a smooth mixture. Season well.

Stuff the vegetables with the mixture, arrange them in a flat roasting pan, cover each one with its little lid and pour around them enough stock to come half-way up their sides. Dot with butter and bake in a moderate oven for forty-five minutes or until they are well cooked through and soft, but have not lost their shape. Serve them hot as they are, sprinkled with roughly chopped dill and parsley.

**Dolma Içi Zeytinyağlı** RICE STUFFING FOR VEGETABLES

This stuffing is used for aubergines, peppers, tomatoes and courgettes. It is made with olive oil and served as a *cold* vegetable dish.

*½ lb rice*
*½ cup olive oil*
*1 cup water*
*1 large tomato*
*1 medium onion*
*1 oz pine nuts*
*1 oz currants*
*1 dessertspoon sugar*
*A pinch of thyme*
*A few sprigs dill and parsley*
*Salt and pepper*

Slice the onion very finely, skin and roughly chop the tomato and wash the rice until the water runs clear. Heat the olive oil in a deep pot and fry the onion until it becomes soft. Add the tomato, nuts, currants, sugar, thyme and season and then stir in the drained rice and fry them together for two or three minutes. Cover with just enough water to come half an inch above the level of the rice and then boil out the water and steam for a few minutes until the rice mixture is dry. Allow to cool. Prepare, stuff and bake the vegetables in the same way as described in the *etli dolma* (above), but omit the butter. After baking allow them to cool in their pan and then serve them cold sprinkled with finely chopped parsley and dill.

# *Pastry, Bread and Sandwiches*

## Börekler: Turkish Pastry

These savoury or sweet pastries known as *böreks* are made with very fine sheets of pastry called *yufka*, which are literally paper thin. There are two main types of *börek*, one which looks like mille-feuilles, and has a filling between the middle layers, and another variety in which the filling is wrapped up in the sheets of pastry into different shapes and sizes. *Börek* get their individual names from the patterns into which they are formed. The wrapped sort can be either baked or fried, and they are usually arranged on large trays. The mille-feuilles variety are baked in a hot oven.

Although in Turkey many cooks buy their *yufka* pastry ready-made and it can also be bought from the special Middle Eastern supply shops in London, there are several recipes for making *yufka* at home, and I find them not only easier to manage but fresher than the bought ones.

The fillings can be cheese, mince meat or spinach for the savoury and nuts, apples, or dried fruits in the sweet. I have given recipes for the savoury ones on pages 111–12 and for the sweet ones on pages 139–40.

### Yufka

PLAIN YUFKA PASTRY

1 *lb flour*
2 *teaspoons salt*
*About ½ pint cold water*

Sift the flour and salt together in a large basin and slowly add enough water to give you a smooth moist dough. Knead this dough for about ten minutes until it feels springy. Form it into balls about the size of a lemon. Flour the end of the kitchen table and roll out each ball as thinly as you can until it looks almost like paper. The Turks use a special long dowl for this which is very thin, but the long handle of a wooden spoon will do. Keep moving the pastry round so that it does not stick and be careful not to stretch it. When you have made all your sheets, put them in a floured towel and store them in a cool place until you are ready to use them.

**Burma Börek** MEAT PASTY

Cut up the *yufka* into three-inch squares, put a little meat mixture (page 111) into the centre and fold up into small bundles tucking the sides well in. Brush with beaten egg and bake in a hot oven (400) for twenty minutes or until nicely browned. Serve hot with pickles.

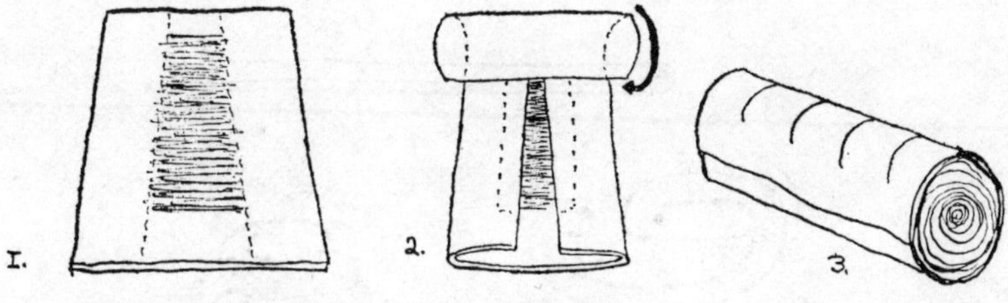


**Sigara Böreği** CIGARETTES

Spread the *yufka* sheets with a mixture of beaten egg and water and cut them into rectangles about three and a half by two and a half inches. Put a filling (pages 111–12) along one edge and fold the sides into the centre and roll up like a cigarette. They should be quite thin and small. Fry them in hot deep oil until they are crisp and drain on absorbent paper. They can be eaten hot or cold and are often served with morning coffee or a drink.

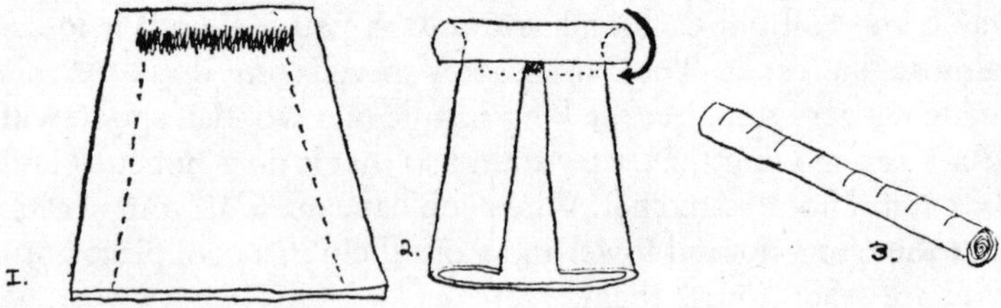


**Kol Böreği** COIL SHAPES

Spread whole *yufka* sheets with melted butter and put a filling (pages 111–12) along one edge. Roll up the entire *yufka* into a roll and arrange on a tray in a coil shape, like a snail. Fill up a whole tray with these neatly arranged in a pleasing pattern and brush with beaten egg. Bake them in a hot oven (400) for thirty minutes until brown. Serve with a salad or pickles.

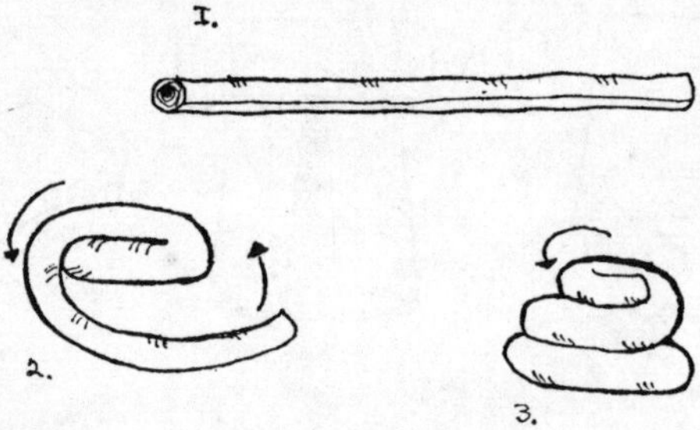


**Tepsi Böreği** TRAY PASTRY

Cut up enough *yufka* to make six sheets that will each cover a large baking tray. Brush each sheet with melted butter and lay three of them on the tray one on top of the other. Now spread one of the savoury fillings on pages 111–12 over the third sheet and cover with three more buttered sheets. Brush the top with beaten egg and bake in a hot oven (400) for thirty minutes or until brown and crisp. This large tray *börek* is served as it is on the tray and makes a good meal. A tomato sauce could accompany it.

**Puf Böreği** FLAKEY YUFKA PASTRY

*1 lb flour*
*2 teaspoons salt*
*1 egg yolk*
*¼ cup olive oil*
*Cold water*
*4 oz margarine*
*Deep oil for frying*

Sift the flour and the salt together in a large bowl and add the egg-yolk and the quarter-cup of olive oil and enough water to make a moist dough. Knead it well and roll it out and fold it over several times. Now break off pieces the size of a lemon and roll each out to about the size of a dinner plate. When all the dough is rolled out like this, spread melted margarine over each layer and press each one on top of the other. Now roll out firmly again and continue rolling until you have one large piece as thin as possible. Cut up the pastry into four-inch squares and fill with any of the fillings given on pages 111–12, and fold or roll into *small* triangles. Fry them in deep hot oil until they are brown. Serve immediately.

ANOTHER RECIPE

*1 lb flour*
*2 ozs melted butter*
*3 eggs*
*Pinch of salt*
*Cold water*

Beat the eggs in a basin and add the melted butter. Mix in the flour and salt gradually and add enough cold water to form a dough. Knead for five minutes until thoroughly mixed and then roll out as thinly as possible into one whole sheet.

**Yoğurtlu Böreği** YOGURT PASTRY

*8 ozs margarine*
*2 tablespoons olive oil*
*1 egg*
*½ pint yogurt*
*A pinch of salt*
*A pinch of bicarbonate of soda*
*Enough flour to make a stiffish dough*

Melt the margarine and mix into it the olive oil, the egg and the yogurt. Gradually add the flour with the salt and soda to this mixture. Work it with the hands until you get a dough which should be kneaded for five minutes and then rolled out to the thickness of a coin. Cut into three-inch rounds to form pasties. They can be filled with a meat or vegetable mixture or cheese and eggs (see pages 111–12). Fold over to close and brush with beaten egg and bake in a hot oven (400) for twenty minutes.

**Su Böreği** WATER PASTRY FROM MALATYA

This type of pastry gets its name because one has to dip it in water before using it. The word 'su' means water.

*3 eggs (this amount can be increased as needed)*
*As much flour as the eggs will take to make a stiff dough*
*½ teaspoon salt*

Beat the eggs in a large bowl and gradually add to them the sifted flour and salt until you have a manageable dough. Knead the dough very thoroughly and form it into one large piece. Flour the end of the kitchen table and roll out the pastry as large and as thin as possible using a long thin dowel. Divide it into about ten sheets.

Have ready a large pot of boiling water and beside it a basin of cold water. Keeping aside two sheets which will not be dipped in the water, take up each sheet on the stick and dip it quickly into the boiling water and then into the cold water and lay it out on to a cloth to dry.

Grease a roasting tin with margarine and lay one of the undipped sheets on it. Brush this well with melted margarine and then lay on four dipped sheets, each being brushed with margarine as it is laid on. Now add one of the fillings (see below). Lay on four more dipped sheets as above, ending up with the second undipped sheet. Brush the top with melted margarine and bake in a hot oven (400) for half an hour.

## Fillings for Yufka pastries

MEAT

1 *lb minced lamb*
1 *medium onion*
*A few sprigs parsley*
*Salt and pepper*

Slice the onion finely and fry in a little butter until soft. Add the mince and chopped parsley and cook until dry and season well.

CHEESE

½ *lb soft white cheese*
1 *egg*
*A few sprigs parsley*
*Salt and pepper*

Beat the egg into the cheese together with the finely chopped parsley and seasoning and combine thoroughly.

SPINACH

1 *lb spinach, or* 1 *tin*
1 *medium onion*
1 *egg*
2 *ozs soft white cheese*
2 *ozs butter*
*Salt and pepper*

Slice the onion finely and fry it in the butter; when it begins to get soft add the washed, roughly chopped spinach and fry until it is just cooked. Cool a little, then add the cheese, egg and seasoning.

MARROW

| | |
|---|---|
| 1 *lb marrow* | *A few leaves mint* |
| 2 *eggs* | *Salt and pepper* |
| 4 *ozs soft white cheese* | |

Peel and grate the marrow and press out as much water as possible. Beat into it the eggs, cheese, mint and seasoning.

Other fillings can be made with meat, potatoes and any vegetable that is not too wet.

## Pide

FLAT BREADS

*Pide* is a type of flat yeast bread which is baked in loaves about the size of a dinner plate and not much higher than one inch. The nearest thing I have seen to it is a Yorkshire oven flat: I have made these oven flats from an ordinary yeast bread dough and they are quite satisfactory. One splits them open and you have something very close to *pide*. *Pide* is used as a basis for many savoury dishes and forms a cheap and popular meal or snack.

There are many little restaurants or *lokanta* which specialize in *pide* dishes, and one can order *pide* with lamb *kebabs*, or mince *köftes* or slices of *döner kebab*, and they will come with a sauce of yogurt and paprika poured over them, accompanied by some hot peppers and tomatoes.

Another variety of *pide* is the toasted *pide*, on which have been melted different fillings such as spinach, cheese, aubergines, eggs, mince, tomatoes, sardines, etc. This sort resembles pizza and are easy to make in an oven.

A very common variety of *pide*, sold by the street vendors in the squares and markets, is a much thinner type resembling a chappati, on which is spread a hot sauce made with chillies, tomatoes, garlic and thyme. The *pide* is then rolled up to make it easier to eat. It is very pleasant to stroll around the shady squares eating one of these. Little boys will come and sell you a glass of water, which they know you will need after eating the hot *pide*!

*1 lb plain white flour*
*1 teaspoon salt*
*½ oz fresh yeast or ¼ oz (1 heaped teaspoon) dry yeast*
*1 teaspoon sugar*
*½ pint lukewarm milk*
*2 ozs margarine*

Warm the sifted flour and salt in a large basin. Dissolve the yeast and sugar in a little of the warm milk. Rub the margarine into the flour and then make a hole in the centre. Pour the dissolved yeast into the hole together with the rest of the milk. Mix from the rim into the centre, gradually taking up the liquid until you have a dough which should then be kneaded for about five minutes until it feels elastic in texture. Form it into a lump and leave to rise in a warm place, which will take about forty minutes. When it is twice its size, knead again until it is back to its original size once more. Form it into flat plate-shaped slabs on a baking sheet and allow to rise again, which will be to about one inch high. Bake the slabs in a hot oven (425) for twenty minutes or until they feel springy and are slightly browned. When they have cooled, split open and use as *pide*.

**Simit** TURKISH CROISSANT WITH SESAME SEEDS

*8 ozs flour*
*½ teaspoon salt*
*2 ozs margarine*
*1 tablespoon olive oil*
*1 tablespoon milk and a little extra*
*1 tablespoon water*
*1 egg*
*Sesame seeds to sprinkle on top*

Put the flour and salt into a large bowl and make a hole in the middle. Into this hole pour the melted margarine, olive oil, milk, water and the beaten egg. Stirring from the outside into the middle gradually mix all the liquids into the flour until you have a dough. It will feel a bit oily, but is quite manageable.

With floured hands shape the dough into rings about the diameter of a saucer and arrange them on a baking sheet. Brush them over with milk and sprinkle the sesame seeds on them. Bake them in a hot oven (400) for thirty minutes until they are nicely browned.

Simits are sold in the streets on long poles, like quoits, and are very good for breakfast. The children love them.

### Sandviç: Sandwiches

Sandwiches are gradually becoming very popular in Turkey today and it is fascinating to see how they have been adapted to their own distinctly Turkish version. Soft white rolls are usually used and into them can be put a vast array of different fillings: cheese, tomatoes, olives, red and green peppers, meat balls, spiced sausage, salad, eggs, aubergine and fish being only a few from which to choose. The little shops which sell these sandwiches have machines resembling miniature presses, which consist of two hot plates which can be clamped together, toasting and flattening the roll and its filling at the same time. The filling is thus blended into the roll and it comes out hot and brown. These hot sandwiches are eaten with some pickle, accompanied by *ayran*, a watered yogurt drink (see page 158), or fresh lemonade.

Snack bars are springing up all over the large cities and it is now a common sight to see people standing at the counter having a quick meal. These shops also sell ice-cream, and fruit juices and cokes and I have even seen carrot juice being made in a modern liquidizer.

I have noticed a gadget on sale in the shops in England which is rather like the Turkish sandwich machine, except that it is much simpler. It consists of two discs about the size of saucers which are clamped together and between which you put the bread and its filling. It has a long handle so that you can hold it over a fire or gas ring. It makes very good toasted sandwiches and is particularly successful for children to use.

# *Egg Dishes*

## Omlet

OMELETTES

*3 eggs*
*2 or 3 spring onions*
*1 oz butter*
*3 or 4 sprigs parsley*
*Salt and pepper*
*Juice of 1 lemon (optional)*

Chop the parsley very finely and cut the spring onions into sections about half an inch long. Beat the eggs with a tablespoonful of water and add the seasoning. Heat the butter in a heavy-bottomed frying pan and fry the onions until they become an attractive green. Add the eggs and parsley and fry gently; keep folding the edges of the eggs in and tipping the pan so that the liquid egg can run round behind and become cooked. When the omelette is nearly set but still a little moist on top, fold it in half and slip it on to a warm plate and serve at once.

The heat under an omelette should not be too hot whilst cooking, but hot enough to slightly brown the under side without burning it. The Turks serve their omelettes with a squeeze of lemon juice over them, which is pleasant, if not to everyone's taste.

## Prasa Omlet

LEEK OMELETTE

*1 lb leeks*
*8 eggs*
*1 oz butter*
*A few sprigs parsley*
*Salt and pepper*

Clean the leeks in plenty of running water and cut off any coarse green ends. Boil them in salted water until they are just beginning to soften, but are not quite cooked through. Drain them and slice into thin rounds. Beat the eggs with the seasoning. Heat a large heavy frying pan and melt the butter in it. Pour the eggs into the pan and then sprinkle over them the leeks and allow the eggs to set like an omelette. This type of omelette is eaten rather thick, and its circumference will be gauged by the size of the frying pan. Slip out on to a serving dish and sprinkle with finely chopped parsley. A few hot green peppers go well with this dish.

NOTE Spinach can also be cooked as an omelette in this way. It should be washed and roughly chopped and boiled with just the water left on from the washing, and a pinch of salt. Drain it well and press out all the water before adding it to the eggs as above.

### Patatesli Omlet — POTATO OMELETTE

| | |
|---|---|
| 2 *medium potatoes* | *Black pepper* |
| 4 *eggs* | *Paprika* |
| 1 *oz butter* | *A squeeze of lemon juice* |
| *A few sprigs parsley* | *Salt and pepper* |

Cut the peeled potatoes into *very* small cubes and fry in the butter until brown with some salt and pepper. Beat the eggs well with a little water, season and pour over the browned potatoes, adding the finely chopped parsley. Turn down the heat, allowing the omelette to form by turning in the edges and tipping the pan so that the liquid can run in behind. When almost dry on top, fold over in half and slip on to a warm plate and serve at once with a little pinch of paprika or lemon juice, if liked.

NOTE These omelettes can also be made with tomatoes, onions

or green peppers. They should be made the same way as the above recipe, making sure that the vegetables being used are sufficiently cooked before adding the eggs to them.

**Domatesli Yumurta** EGGS WITH TOMATOES

*1 medium onion*
*3 large tomatoes*
*3 eggs or 1 per person*
*1 oz butter*
*A few sprigs parsley*
*Salt and pepper*

Chop the onion very finely and fry it in the butter in a thick frying pan until transparent. Add the skinned and cut up tomatoes, season well and cook gently until soft. Make three depressions and break the eggs into them. Cover and allow the eggs to poach, until the white is cooked but the yolks are still soft. Break the yolks so that they mingle with the tomatoes. Serve at once sprinkled with parsley.

This is also very good with a few green peppers fried with the tomatoes.

Another method of serving this dish is to transfer the tomato mixture when cooked into individual cocotte dishes. Break an egg into each one and bake gently until set. Serve with black pepper.

**Kıymalı Yumurta** EGGS WITH MINCE

*4 eggs*
*½ lb minced lamb or beef*
*4 ozs white cheese*
*1 medium onion*
*Butter for frying*
*A few sprigs parsley*
*Salt and pepper*

Chop the onion very finely and fry it in some butter in a wide frying; pan allow it to become transparent and then add the mince. Turn the meat so that it browns all over and cook until it dries out a bit. Then add the grated or crumbled cheese and stir well with plenty of seasoning. Spread out the mixture, make four little depressions in it and break the eggs into these spaces. Cover the pan and cook gently until the eggs are set. Serve with chopped parsley sprinkled over them or a pinch of paprika.

**İspanaklı Yumurta** EGGS WITH SPINACH

- 1 *lb fresh spinach or* 1 *tin*
- 1 *medium onion*
- 2 *ozs butter*
- 4 *eggs*
- *Salt and pepper*

Cut the onion up very finely and fry in one ounce of butter until transparent. Add the chopped spinach, which should have been well washed. This washing should provide enough water in which to cook the spinach. Season. When the spinach is soft, spread it out well, make four depressions in it and poach the eggs in these until set. A cover helps greatly in the cooking of this dish. Serve at once.

NOTE This dish is also very good made with left-over pilaf, which is heated in some butter and the eggs cooked in the same way as above.

**Çılbır** POACHED EGGS IN YOGURT

This is rather an unusual dish but is surprisingly good and is very useful as an idea for a start to a dinner party, providing everyone likes yogurt.

- 1 *egg for each person*
- ¼ *pint yogurt per person or one carton*
- 2 *cloves garlic*
- 1 *oz butter*
- 1 *teaspoon paprika*
- *Salt and black pepper*

Beat all the yogurt well together and blend in the crushed garlic which should have been pounded in a mortar with a little salt. Divide the yogurt into individual serving dishes.

Now poach the eggs carefully, preferably in some little ramekin dishes standing in boiling water. When set but still very soft, slip carefully into the yogurt. Melt one ounce of butter and stir in a teaspoon of paprika and pour over the yogurt in attractive patterns. Serve at once so that the eggs are still hot in the cold yogurt.

# *Pilafs*

The use of rice was probably introduced into Asia Minor from the east, and like so many dishes from Central Asia, has now become an important part of the Turkish cuisine. Rice is not really an indigenous crop in Turkey and is mostly grown in the south-eastern area of the country. It is quite expensive and considered rather a luxury by the average poor, who rely on wheat and corn for their staple foods. The method of cooking rice known as a pilaf is entirely Turkish and gives us a most delicious and versatile dish in which any amount of variation can be achieved using vegetables, meat, chicken or fish. The pilaf is a method of cooking rice in stock so that the rice absorbs the flavour of the stock and yet the grains remain dry and separate. With the rice can be cooked many different combinations of foods, giving the richness and interest for which these dishes have become so famous.

## Basic Rules for a Plain Pilaf

The plain pilaf can be served as it is with parsley and a little paprika on top. It will go very well with roast lamb or chicken, quails, liver, mussels or prawns, *kebabs köftes*, or any other savoury dish.

Always use good-quality long-grain rice. One cup of dry rice should be enough for four people, but use a little more if they are keen rice eaters.

Always wash the rice very well in cold water. Put the rice

into a pan and cover it with water and then rub the grains between the fingers to get out all the starchy whiteness which tends to make the rice soggy if not removed. Keep pouring off the water and adding fresh until it runs clear. Strain the rice as dry as possible in a sieve, and put aside.

Fry in two ounces of butter a finely sliced onion and simmer it until it is partially cooked. Now add the rice to the onion and stir the butter well into the grains and fry for three minutes more. Add a little crushed garlic at this stage if you like it.

Now add enough meat or vegetable stock to come an inch above the rice level. Season well and add some parsley and allow the rice to boil quickly with the lid off until all the fluid has been absorbed and little holes appear all over the surface of the rice. When you think all the water has gone, turn down the heat to its lowest or draw off the hot plate and cover. Leave the rice to steam for about thirty minutes. It should now be quite cooked and tip out of the pot easily on to a platter.

## Vegetable Pilafs

In these pilafs, the rice and the vegetable are cooked at the same time. Celery, tomatoes, peas, French beans, leeks, aubergines, peppers, mushrooms, onions, nuts, currants and sultanas can all be used either individually or in combinations. Meat and fish can also be cooked in this way.

Adopt exactly the same method as in making the plain pilaf except that the vegetables or meat, which should be cut up fairly small, should be fried in the butter for three or four minutes before adding the washed rice. Then continue as described above.

As well as using nuts such as almonds and pine nuts in the rice, pilafs are often garnished with these nuts fried to a golden brown. A few red peppers or slices of tomato make an attractive finish to the dish.

**Pilâv Tavuklu** CHICKEN PILAF

*1½ cups rice*
*1 roasting chicken*
*1½ pints stock made from the giblets, wings and legs*
*1 medium onion*
*1 medium celery or celeriac*
*1 square green pepper*
*A few sprigs parsley*
*½ pint yogurt*
*2 ozs butter*
*1 tablespoon olive oil*
*Salt and pepper*

Rub the chicken all over with olive oil and salt and roast in the usual way; the oil gives the skin a crisp brownness. Roast for about an hour. Over-cooked chickens lose their flavour.

Prepare the chicken stock and add a chicken cube if you feel the broth is too weak. Wash the rice and put aside. Roughly slice the onion and celery, or celeriac, and seed the pepper which can be cut into fairly thick pieces.

Melt two ounces of butter and fry the onions, celery and the pepper. When they are becoming a little softer, add the rice and fry altogether for three or four minutes. Add enough chicken stock to come about an inch above the level of the rice and cook as described for the plain pilaf.

When the rice is ready, turn it out on to a warm platter, joint the chicken and lay on top and sprinkle with chopped parsley and paprika. Serve with the gravy from the roast chicken and a bowl of warmed, beaten yogurt.

NOTE A teaspoon of turmeric or saffron powder can be added to the rice at the frying stage, and you will have a soft yellow pilaf.

ANOTHER RECIPE

This is another method of cooking chicken with rice.

*1½ cups rice*
*1 roasting chicken*
*1 medium onion*
*2 ozs walnuts*
*4 ozs peas*
*1 pint chicken stock*

*2 ozs butter*
*A few leaves tarragon*
*A few sprigs parsley*
*Salt and pepper*

Cut all the flesh off the chicken and slice it into fine strips with a very sharp knife. Heat the butter in a deep pot, fry the roughly sliced onions until they become transparent and then add the chicken slices. Turn the chicken in the butter and add the tarragon, walnuts, peas and seasoning, and fry for three minutes more before adding the washed rice. Stir the rice into the rest of the ingredients and then add the stock to come to one inch above the chicken and rice. Continue to cook as for the plain pilaf. Tip out on to a warm platter and sprinkle with finely chopped parsley and serve with a bowl of warm yogurt.

**Pilâv Domatesli** PILAF WITH TOMATOES

*1 cup rice*
*4 large tomatoes*
*1 medium onion*
*2 cloves garlic*
*1 pint stock*
*2 ozs butter*
*A pinch dry basil*
*A few sprigs parsley*
*Salt and pepper*

Fry the roughly sliced onion in the butter in a deep pot and when the slices start to turn transparent add the skinned whole tomatoes, crushed garlic, basil, finely chopped parsley and seasoning. Cook for about three minutes before adding the washed rice. Take care not to crush the tomatoes too much when stirring in the rice or the pilaf will be rather mushy. Cover with the chicken stock to one inch above the level of the rice and continue as for a plain pilaf.

NOTE These vegetable pilafs are sometimes wetter than the plain ones and they should never be stirred, as their appearance may be spoiled.

## Pilâv Kuzulu

PILAF WITH LAMB

*1½ cups rice*
*1 lb boneless lamb*
*1 medium onion*
*2 ozs pine nuts*
*1 oz sultanas*
*1 pint stock*
*1 square green pepper*
*A pinch thyme*
*1 teaspoon paprika*
*Butter*
*Salt and pepper*

Cut the lamb into fine two-inch long strips and fry it gently with the roughly-sliced onion in butter. When they begin to brown slightly add the pine nuts, sultanas, thyme, thinly sliced pepper and seasoning and cook for a further three minutes. Stir in the washed rice and continue to fry for three minutes more before adding the stock. Continue as for a plain pilaf.

Tip out on to a warm platter and serve with a bowl of yogurt over which a pinch of paprika has been sprinkled.

NOTE Roast lamb can also be served with a pilaf, in which case it can be piled on top. Insert small pieces of garlic into the meat before roasting it in olive oil, to give it extra flavour.

## Patlıcanlı Pilâv

PILAF WITH AUBERGINES

*1 cup rice*
*2 large round aubergines*
*2 large tomatoes*
*1 large onion*
*1½ pints stock*
*2 ozs butter*
*A few mint leaves*
*Salt and pepper*

Peel the aubergines and cut them into rough one-inch squares; salt them heavily and place them between two plates and leave for twenty minutes. Meanwhile wash the rice, slice the onions roughly and skin the tomatoes. Melt two ounces of butter and fry the onions and then the tomatoes with some salt and pepper. Rinse the aubergines thoroughly and pat dry in a cloth, and add to the other vegetables, turning well to fry all over. Put the washed rice on top and add enough stock or water to come an inch above the level of the rice. Simmer gently until all the water has been absorbed. *Do not stir this pilaf at all*, but shake the pan if necessary. Add a few mint leaves before steaming. When you tip out the pilaf all the vegetables will come up on top. Serve with warm yogurt.

**Karidesli Pilâv** PILAF WITH PRAWNS

1½ *cups rice*
2 *ozs butter*
1 *lb fresh prawns (or cooked ones if fresh are unobtainable)*
1 *medium onion*
2 *cloves garlic*
2 *large tomatoes*
1 *medium celery head or celeriac*
1 *teaspoon saffron or turmeric powder*
1 *pint prawn or fish stock*
1 *lemon*
*A few sprigs parsley*
*Salt*

If the prawns are fresh, take off the outer scales and head and put all the trimmings in some water with salt to make a stock. Do not use the prawns themselves for this. If the prawns are already cooked, make a fish stock with some other fish.

Melt the two ounces of butter and fry the prawns with a little salt until they are done on each side. This will only take a minute or two; then remove them and keep them warm. Now fry the finely sliced onion and crushed garlic in the same butter, and add the skinned tomatoes and finely sliced celery. When they are a little soft, add the saffron or turmeric powder and then the washed rice and stir well. Cover with the fish stock and cook out the liquid. When the steaming stage is reached, lay the prawns on top of the rice and cover and steam for a further twenty minutes. Serve with slices of lemon laid on top of the pilaf.

NOTE Mussels, octopus, squid, crab, oysters, salted cod or herring, smoked eels, cockles, crayfish, scallops etc. can all be cooked with a pilaf in the same way.

## Iç Pilâv

A SAVOURY PILAF

| | |
|---|---|
| 1½ *cups rice* | 2 *ozs pine nuts* |
| 3 *ozs butter* | 2 *ozs almonds* |
| ½ *lb lamb's liver* | 2 *ozs sultanas* |
| 1 *medium onion* | 1 *pint stock* |
| 2 *large tomatoes* | *A few sprigs parsley and sage* |
| 1 *medium celery head or celeriac* | *Salt and pepper* |

Cut the liver into thin inch-long strips and fry it gently in one ounce of butter, with some salt and pepper. Do not over-cook the liver; it will be ready when the blood starts to come to the surface. Lay aside. In a deep pot fry the finely sliced onion in the rest of the butter together with the skinned tomatoes, finely sliced celery, nuts and sultanas and chopped sage. Stir in the washed rice and add enough stock to come one inch above the level of the rice and then allow the stock to boil out. Place the liver strips on top of the rice and steam for a further twenty minutes. Tip out and garnish with finely chopped parsley.

## Bulgur Pilâvı

PILAF WITH WHEAT

| | |
|---|---|
| 2 *cups bulgur* | 2 *pints good stock* |
| 1 *large onion* | 2 *hot long green peppers* |
| 4 *ozs butter* | *Salt and pepper* |

Slice the onion finely and fry it in the butter in a heavy deep pot until it becomes transparent; add the dry *bulgur* and stir it into the butter until it bubbles, then add the stock and seasoning and continue stirring until all the liquid has been absorbed and the wheat is soft. Serve hot with green peppers to garnish.

# *Salads*

If possible, salads are eaten at nearly every meal, even if it is only a few hot peppers or a tomato. The combination of salad and yogurt is a pleasant remedy against the heat as well as being extremely healthy. The Turks seemed to have developed naturally well-balanced meals by instinct rather than dietary theory.

Cucumbers, tomatoes and lettuces are plentiful and cheap. The most usual dressing is lemon juice and olive oil with a little salt and parsley. Cos lettuce is a favourite variety and one often sees someone consuming a whole cos at one go. Slabs of salty goat's cheese are another common start to a meal, usually with some black olives. This rather pungent cheese arrives in the markets packed into actual goat skins, still black and hairy, in which apparently it keeps better.

It is the arrangement of the salads, rather than their ingredients, which make them characteristically Turkish. Tremendous trouble is taken to see that the food is served with colourful contrasts and in attractive patterns.

**Cacık** CUCUMBERS IN YOGURT

*1 cucumber*
*½ pint yogurt*
*A pinch of salt*
*A few drops of vinegar*
*A few drops of olive oil*

Peel and slice the cucumber into small bits. Beat the yogurt with a little salt and a few drops of vinegar and olive oil. Put the cucumber bits into a small bowl and mix the yogurt into it and serve very cold.

This is a very refreshing dish on a hot day.

**Fasulye Piyaz** HARICOT BEANS IN OIL

*½ lb haricot beans*
*2 cloves garlic*
*2 tablespoons olive oil*
*1 tablespoon vinegar*
*Pinch of sugar*
*Salt and pepper*
*Juice of 1 lemon*
*2 or 3 sprigs parsley*

Soak the beans overnight in plenty of water. Throw this water away and put the beans into fresh cold water to which has been added half a teaspoon of salt and simmer them until they are soft but not broken or mushy. Strain the beans, put them into a bowl and mix into them, while still hot, the crushed garlic, olive oil, vinegar, sugar and salt and pepper to taste. Stir these well into the beans and then allow them to cool. Serve cold with finely chopped parsley on top and the lemon juice which should be squeezed over the beans just before eating.

NOTE This dish can also be served garnished with black olives, sliced tomatoes, hard-boiled eggs and sliced green peppers, which makes a pleasant variation.

**Patlıcan Salatası** AUBERGINE SALAD

*3 large round aubergines*
*¼ pint olive oil*
*Juice of 1 lemon*
*¼ pint yogurt*
*2 cloves garlic*
*½ teaspoon salt*

For the garnish:
*2 tomatoes*
*1 green pepper*
*4 ozs black or green olives*
*1 small mild onion*
*A few sprigs parsley*

Bake or grill the aubergines until the skin is black and the flesh feels soft inside. This is usually done on the top of a stove, by putting the aubergine directly on to the hot plate or gas ring and turning it over until all the skin is burnt and it feels very soft inside. Hold the aubergine in a cloth and slit open one side and scoop out all the flesh into a basin. Squeeze the lemon juice over it immediately to prevent discoloration. Mash the aubergine with the yogurt, crushed garlic, salt and olive oil until you have a smooth purée. Pour the purée into a dish and garnish with sliced skinned tomatoes, sliced peppers, olives and the finely sliced onions. Sprinkle over the finely chopped parsley and serve chilled.

### Patlıcan Yoğurtlu — AUBERGINES IN YOGURT

*3 long or 2 round aubergines*
*½ pint yogurt*
*2 cloves garlic*
*3 tablespoons olive oil*
*½ teaspoon caraway seeds*
*A few sprigs dill*
*Salt*

Wipe the aubergines and peel and slice them into fairly thin rings, immediately sprinkle thickly with salt and place between two plates; leave for twenty minutes so that the bitter juices can be drawn out by the salt. Meanwhile beat the yogurt with the crushed garlic, a little salt and the caraway seeds.

Rinse the aubergines very thoroughly and pat dry in a cloth. Fry them in the hot oil until they are brown on both sides and quite soft. Arrange them on a dish and pour the yogurt sauce over them and garnish with a little fresh dill.

### Patates Salatası — POTATO SALAD

*4 medium potatoes*
*2 large tomatoes*
*2 cloves garlic*
*Juice of 1 lemon*
*1 tablespoon olive oil*
*2 or 3 sprigs parsley*
*Black pepper*
*Salt*

Boil the potatoes in their skins until tender but not too soft and allow to cool. Skin them and cut into small cubes. Wash the tomatoes and cut into quarters then cut these in half again and mix them with the potatoes taking care not to get them mushy. Mix the crushed garlic with a little salt and the olive oil and lemon juice, finely chopped parsley and black pepper and pour this over the potatoes. Cool well before serving.

**Pancar Salatası** BEETROOT SALAD

*4 beetroot*
*½ pint yogurt*
*2 cloves garlic*
*A few caraway seeds*
*A pinch paprika*
*Salt and pepper*

Boil the beets in plenty of salty water for about two hours. Cool, and rub off the skin carefully without breaking the flesh too much. It should come off easily if the beets have been boiled sufficiently. Slice and arrange on a dish and sprinkle with salt and pepper. Beat the yogurt with the crushed garlic and a little salt and the caraway seeds and pour it over the beets. Sprinkle with paprika.

**Yumurta Salatası** EGG SALAD

*4 hard-boiled eggs*
*1 medium onion*
*1 tablespoon olive oil*
*Juice of 1 lemon*
*A few sprigs parsley*
*A pinch of sugar*
*Salt and pepper*

Slice the hard-boiled eggs and arrange them on a serving dish. Slice the onion very finely and lay the slices on top of the eggs. Mix together the olive oil, lemon juice, finely chopped parsley and the sugar and seasoning and pour it over the eggs.

**Domates Salatası** TOMATO SALAD

Tomato salad is perhaps the most popular salad of all, and

accompanies practically every meal. This is partly due to the very tasty and juicy large tomatoes grown in Turkey which have a strong flavour and are a joy to eat. They are thinly sliced and laid in a neat row down the centre of an oval serving dish. On one side of the tomatoes one puts a row of black olives and on the other side some green peppers. Parsley is sprinkled over the top and a dressing of lemon juice, olive oil, salt and pepper is poured over all. It should be quite wet. Any left over juice is mopped up with thick hunks of bread.

# *Yogurt, Sauces and Pickles*

## Yogurt

Yogurt forms a very important dairy food in Turkey, where it is difficult to keep milk fresh in hot weather and where most people do not have private refrigerators. Their ancestors dealt with the problem quite satisfactorily by making a curd which will last for many days and actually improves in flavour with keeping. From this curd can also be made cheese. Yogurt is made by adding the bacillus Bulgarius to milk warmed to blood temperature. The milk must remain warm for about twelve hours to form the curd. The Turkish housewife simply puts a large earthenware basin of yogurt in the sun, covered with a cloth, and the yogurt forms throughout the day. In the winter it must be kept warm near a stove. It is extremely nourishing, good for the digestion, and a delicious addition to most dishes. Home-made yogurt is both cheaper and tastes better than the bought variety in countries outside the Middle East, where it is plentiful everywhere. In Turkey yogurt is spelt *yoğurt* with a silent 'g' and the syllables are more slurred together than in English.

The simplest method of keeping the milk warm for twelve hours is to put it in a thermos flask. The wide-mouthed variety is best for this, but an ordinary one will do just as well.

Boil your milk (as much as will fit in the thermos) for two minutes, stirring to prevent rising. Cool in a basin and wait until you can put your finger in the milk without pain. This is the right temperature. Add one teaspoon of live yogurt to the milk and stir it well in. Pour the warm milk into the thermos and close the lid. Leave overnight and the yogurt will be ready the next day. Tip it out carefully into a dish and scrape around the thermos with a wooden spoon. A metal spoon is liable to break the thermos. Keep the yogurt cool or put it in the refrigerator. It improves in flavour in about two days, and will become thicker. The first batch is sometimes a bit runny, but it will become thicker as each batch is made. The best yogurt will be achieved in about a week.

Live yogurt, in which the bacillus has not been sterilized, can be bought from most health-food shops. In the branded yogurts, the bacillus has usually been killed and this renders them useless for re-making. As soon as one can get a 'starter', one can make yogurt indefinitely.

The thermos flask and bowls should be scalded between use, to keep each lot of yogurt fresh.

## Sauces and Pickles

Many dishes have sauces over them; but some are served with a little dish of sauce beside the plate. Pickles, paprika and black pepper are served with most meals. Hot butter with paprika stirred into it and a hot yogurt sauce are the most common garnishes, together with parsley and hot peppers. If cold yogurt is served it will be in a bowl of its own and one can spoon it over the dish as one fancies.

In the sauces given here I have used only Turkish recipes, but this does not mean that the more well-known sauces such as béchamel, hollandaise, gravies, capers and white roux sauces are not used in Turkish cooking. However, the nut and garlic sauces form a large and characteristic part of the Turkish kitchen and are both interesting and unusual.

### Terbiye — LEMON AND EGG SAUCE

*2 eggs*
*Juice of 1 lemon*
*Mild white stock*
*Salt and pepper*

Beat the eggs, and add the lemon juice gradually and continue beating. Season and add about two tablespoons of stock (which should not be too hot) and mix well together with a fork.

NOTE This sauce can be added to soups, vegetables, tripe, *köftes*, etc. It is an extremely common combination in Turkish cooking.

**Salca Yumurtalı** EGG SAUCE WITH GARLIC

*3 or 4 cloves garlic*
*1 egg*
*Juice of 1 lemon*
*A little olive oil*
*Salt*

Pound the garlic in a mortar with a pinch of salt. Beat the eggs in a bowl and then gradually add to them the garlic and lemon juice and olive oil a few drops at a time until the sauce becomes smooth and thick. It must be continuously beaten while adding the olive oil and will take about five minutes to reach the right consistency.

**Limon Salçası** LEMON SAUCE

*Juice of 1 lemon*
*1 tablespoon olive oil*
*3 or 4 sprigs parsley*
*Salt and black pepper*

Chop the parsley very finely and put it into a bowl together with the lemon juice and olive oil, salt and pepper. Beat it with a fork until it is thoroughly blended.

NOTE This sauce is used for fish and omelettes, in salads, and over practically any dish that is being served cold.

**Tarator** GARLIC AND WALNUT SAUCE

*3 cloves garlic*
*4 ozs walnuts*
*2 normal slices bread*

| | |
|---|---|
| 2 *tablespoons vinegar or lemon juice* | 1 *tablespoon olive oil* |
| | *Salt* |

Blanche the walnuts to remove the skin and put them through a fine mincer, then pound them in a mortar together with the garlic and some salt. Soak the bread in a little water and squeeze out and crumble into the mixture. Add the oil drop by drop and the vinegar or lemon juice until you have a smooth thick sauce. Serve on a little dish beside each plate.

NOTE This sauce is very good with fried mussels, fish, aubergine, courgettes and chicken. It is the basis for the Circassian chicken sauce but when used in that dish it is thinned by adding chicken broth to it.

**Tarator Çamfistıklı** PINE NUT SAUCE

| | |
|---|---|
| 3 *ozs pine nuts* | *Juice of* 1 *lemon* |
| 2 *cloves garlic* | 1 *teaspoon salt* |
| *A little olive oil* | |

Put the pine nuts through a mincer and then pound them well in a mortar with a teaspoon of salt and the garlic. Add the oil drop by drop until you have a smooth thick sauce which can be thinned with the lemon juice.

**Tarator Sade** GARLIC SAUCE

| | |
|---|---|
| 3 *or* 4 *cloves garlic* | *Juice of* 1 *lemon* |
| 1 *teaspoon salt* | *A little olive oil* |

Pound the garlic and salt together in a mortar. Gradually add the olive oil drop by drop and then the lemon juice until you have a thickish sauce.

NOTE This sauce can accompany any dish that will go well with garlic. It is particularly good with vegetables and sea food.

**Domates Salçası** TOMATO SAUCE

| | |
|---|---|
| 2 *ozs butter* | *A few sprigs parsley* |
| 1 *small onion* | *A pinch basil* |
| 2 *cloves garlic* | 1 *bay leaf* |
| 4 *or* 5 *large tomatoes or* 1 *tin* | *Salt and pepper* |
| 1 *green pepper* | |

Chop up the onion very finely and fry it gently in the butter. When it is becoming soft, add the skinned and chopped tomatoes and the seeded pepper cut up into small pieces. Add the crushed garlic and all the seasoning and simmer for about ten minutes. Over-cooking spoils the delicate flavour of the tomatoes. Sieve and keep warm.

A PLAIN TOMATO PURÉE

This can be used when adding to a dish which calls for tomato purée.

Simmer three or four skinned, chopped tomatoes in a little butter, add one clove of crushed garlic, salt and pepper and a little basil. Sieve and use as required.

**Turşu** PICKLES

These family pickles are made in great quantities during the summer months when the vegetables are cheap and they are packed into large earthenware jars to last the year. The quantities I was given seemed enough to supply an army but I was assured that this was for an ordinary family. The quantities I give here are far more modest.

| | |
|---|---|
| 1 *lb large tomatoes* | 4 *cloves garlic* |
| 1 *lb cucumbers* | *Vinegar* |
| 1 *lb green peppers* (*the long variety which are quite hot*) | 1 *teaspoon salt per jar* |

Wash the vegetables, skin the tomatoes, peel the cucumbers, and seed the peppers. Cut them up into largish pieces about two inches square, pack into half-pound jars and add one teaspoon of salt to each jar. Cover with the vinegar and tie down the jar covers. Store in a cool place until the vegetables go yellow, when they will be ready to eat.

**Lahana Turşusu** PICKLED CABBAGE

Cut up the cabbage and cook it in a little water to soften it. A few minutes should be long enough. Pack it into jars and add one teaspoon of salt to each jar and cover with vinegar.

**Yeşil Biber Turşusu** SWEET PEPPER PICKLE

Cut peppers or chillies into rings and take out all the seeds. If the seeds are left in, the pickle will be very hot indeed. The long peppers are not as hot as little chillies, and this pickle can be made with either. Pack them into jars and cover with white vinegar, one teaspoon of salt and two dessertspoons of sugar. A small glass of sherry mixed with the vinegar is good, but this is entirely optional.

NOTE This pickle goes very well with *pilâv* and *köftes*.

**Patlıcan Turşusu** AUBERGINE PICKLE

2 *lbs aubergines* (*or as many as required*)
1 *celery*
¼ *lb carrots*
2 *red chillies*
6 *cloves garlic*
10 *sprigs parsley*
*Vinegar*
*Salt*

Parboil the aubergines whole and then press out of them as much water as possible. Cut the aubergines into quarters, and chop the carrots and celery into pieces about an inch long. Seed the chillies and roughly pull the parsley into bits. Pack them together into a large jar and cover with the vinegar and a generous amount of salt. Leave in a cool place for at least a fortnight.

# *Sweets and Sweet Pastries*

### Baklava: Mille-Feuilles Sweet Pastry

In these recipes the same *yufka* pastry is used that is mentioned in the pastry section (page 106).

### Traditional Baklava

These large flat pastries are baked on a tray or baking sheet. Cut sixteen sheets of *yufka* to fit your tray and arrange them in two sets of eight each. Grease the tray with butter, and have ready about four ounces of melted butter or margarine in a cup. Dip your pastry brush in the butter and spread generously over each sheet of *yufka* before laying it on the tray. Lay on the first eight sheets in this fashion and then put in the filling which should consist of enough chopped walnuts to cover the *yufka* and plenty of melted butter, and then cover with the rest of the *yufka* sheets in the same way. Now cut through all the layers carefully with a sharp knife making oblique cuts across from both sides so that you produce diamond shapes. Bake in a hot oven (400) for about twenty minutes until crisp and brown. While still hot, you can pour over the pastry a syrup made with six ounces of sugar and half a pint of water, although some people prefer to eat *baklava* crisp with icing sugar sprinkled on top. Serve with thick or clotted cream.

### Sarı Burma

Take four sheets of *yufka* as large as you can handle, and brush each one with melted butter and lay them one on top of the other. Cover one half of the top sheet with chopped walnuts and almonds and roll up like a Swiss roll. Brush the top with more butter and bake in a hot oven (400) for twenty minutes until brown and crisp. While still hot soak with syrup or sprinkle with icing sugar.

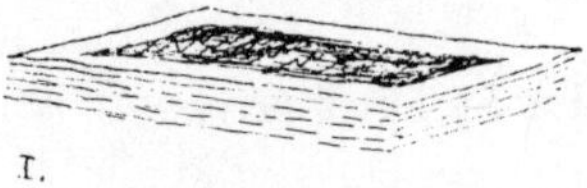

1.

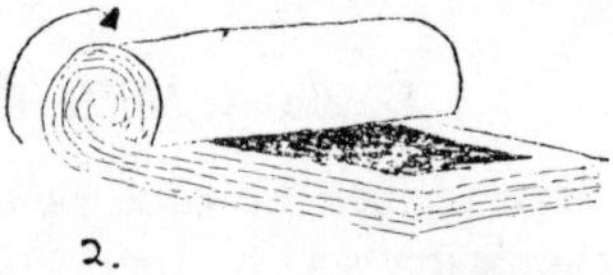

2.

3.

**Elmalı Börek** PASTRIES FILLED WITH APPLES

Spread out three sheets of *yufka* and brush with melted butter. Cut into two-inch strips and put a teaspoonful of the following mixture in the centre and fold into triangles by folding over and over from side to side.

Mixture:
2 *apples chopped up very small*
*A pinch cinnamon*
1 *oz sugar*
2 *ozs chopped nuts consisting of almonds, walnuts and pine-nuts*
*Lemon juice to moisten*
*Butter*

Brush with butter and bake on a hot oven (400) for about twenty minutes or until brown and crisp. These are especially good if sprinkled with icing sugar.

This filling can also be used for a large roll and in that case use six sheets of buttered *yufka* and roll up like a Swiss roll and bake for about half an hour.

NOTE The bought *yufka* are extremely thin and are rather tricky to handle. For the *böreks* I find a home-made *yufka* much easier to manage (see page 106).

### Hanım Parmağı

LADIES' FINGERS

- 5 *ozs margarine*
- ¾ *pint water*
- 6 *ozs flour*
- 4 *eggs*
- 6 *ozs sugar*
- *Olive oil for deep frying*

Melt the margarine in three-quarters of a pint of water, and carefully add the flour to this, stirring all the time. Cook it gently for about fifteen minutes. Take it off the stove and when it becomes lukewarm beat in the eggs. Take out spoonfuls and roll into shapes like fingers about two and a half inches long. When they are all ready, fry them in hot deep oil until they are brown. Drain them on absorbent paper and arrange on a large plate. Make a thick syrup with six ounces of sugar and half a pint of water, and when this is cool pour it over the fingers and serve them while still warm.

### Kadın Göbeği

DIMPLE CAKES *or* LADIES' NAVELS

- 1 *lb flour*
- 4 *ozs butter*
- 4 *ozs sugar*
- 4 *eggs*
- ¼ *pint milk*
- *Clotted cream known as kaymak in Turkey and resembling Devonshire cream in consistency*

Soften the butter and beat in the sugar until it is light and fluffy. Continue beating and gradually add the eggs and flour. Moisten with a little milk if necessary, but keep the dough fairly stiff. Form into balls about the size of an orange, and make a depression in the top of each one with the back of your fingers. Arrange them on a baking sheet and bake in a moderate oven until they are lightly browned. Pour over them a syrup, so that they become spongy, but not sodden and put a blob of thick cream in each dimple. These cakes are known as ladies' navels. One can imagine why.

**Saray Lokması** PALACE SWEET FRITTERS

1 *pint yogurt*
8 *ozs flour*
2 *eggs*
*A pinch of bicarbonate of soda*
*Olive oil for deep frying*
*Caster sugar*

Beat the eggs and yogurt well together in a basin. Gradually add the flour and bicarbonate of soda, beating all the time. Heat the oil to smoking hot and drop in little teaspoonfuls of the mixture and fry until they are golden-brown. Drain them well on some absorbent paper and then roll them in caster sugar. They are eaten hot, dipped into thick cream.

**Yoğurt Tatlısı** YOGURT CAKE

1 *pint yogurt*
3 *eggs*
12 *ozs flour*
8 *ozs sugar*
1 *teaspoon baking powder*
*A pinch salt*
*Juice of* 1 *lemon*

Put the eggs in a large basin and beat them, while adding the yogurt. Continue beating and gradually add six ounces of sugar and the flour, baking powder and salt. When they are all well combined, tip into a greased and floured cake tin and bake in a moderate oven (350) for one hour.

Make a syrup with six ounces of sugar and half a pint of water and the lemon juice. When it has become thick, pour it over the cake and return the cake to the oven for a further few minutes so that the syrup can soak into it. Serve hot with cream. One can also serve this cake with hot thick jam which can be poured over the cake instead of the syrup in the same way.

**Vişne Ekmeği** TURKISH BREAD PUDDING WITH CHERRIES

*6 thin slices stale white bread*
*Butter to spread*
*4 ozs sugar*
*1 lb Morello cherries*
*2 cups water*

Trim off the crusts from the bread and spread with plenty of butter; cut into quarters and arrange in a pie or pudding dish. Bake in a moderate oven (350) until slightly golden. Meanwhile stone the cherries and cook with the sugar and water until syrupy. Pour over the bread and bake again until most of the liquid is absorbed. Serve with thick cream.

NOTE Morello cherries are very plentiful in Turkey, but any cherries in season would do for this dish. Even tinned cherries could be used, in which case omit the syrup unless they are unsweetened ones.

**Lokum** TURKISH DELIGHT

*2 lbs sugar*
*1 pint water*
*4 ozs cornstarch flour*
*1 teaspoon cream of tartar*
*¼ pint liquid fruit juice (grape, orange, lemon, grapefruit, rose petal)*
*A few drops cochineal, for colour*
*Icing sugar and coconut for rolling in*

Put the sugar and water into a large pot and boil for about forty minutes or until it becomes syrupy. Meanwhile mix the cornstarch with the fruit juice and cream of tartar. When the syrup is ready, pour the cornstarch mixture gradually into the syrup, which should be boiling all the time, and stir continuously. Boil for another twenty minutes until it becomes slightly thicker. It takes a bit of trial and error to gauge when the mixture is ready. If it boils too long it will turn out hard like toffee, and if it is too soft it will not keep its shape when cool. It should feel soft but firm after cooling. Add some cochineal if you would like a pink colour. Pour the mixture out into a square cake tin which has been lined with very slightly oiled paper. When cool cut into squares and roll in icing sugar and coconut, if liked, and store in a tin. It will keep for ages.

**Çilek Reçeli** STRAWBERRY JAM

2 *lbs strawberries*
2 *lbs sugar*
*Juice of* 1 *lemon*

Crush the strawberries slightly and boil gently with the lemon juice. Add the sugar and stir until dissolved. Boil briskly, stirring all the time, for ten minutes. Pour into sterilized jars and cover with melted wax.

**Kayısı Reçeli** APRICOT JAM

3 *cups dried apricots*
2½ *cups water*
2 *cups sugar*
½ *cup almonds*

Soak the apricots overnight in the water. Cook in the same water over a low heat for thirty minutes. Add the sugar and skinned almonds and cook quickly until set. These quantities will make one quart.

**İrmik Helvası** SEMOLINA WITH ALMONDS

4 *ozs semolina*
2 *ozs butter*
6 *ozs almonds*
1½ *pints milk*
4 *ozs sugar*
*A few drops of vanilla essence or a vanilla pod*

Soak the almonds in boiling water for about ten minutes so that the skins will slip off easily. Melt the butter and fry the almonds, then add the dry semolina and cook gently, stirring all the time, until the semolina and almonds are nicely browned and give off an almond smell. This takes about twenty minutes.

In a separate pan boil the milk and sugar and then add the vanilla essence or pod. When the semolina is ready add the milk to it (having removed the pod) and stir until thickened. If it seems too thick add a little more milk. Serve slightly warmed with cream.

**Revani** SEMOLINA CAKE WITH SYRUP

8 *ozs semolina*
8 *small eggs*
8 *ozs sugar*
*Rind of* 1 *lemon*
1 *teaspoon baking powder*
*A pinch salt*
½ *pint water*

For the syrup:

6 *ozs sugar*
½ *pint water*

Separate the eggs into two basins. Beat the yolks with the eight ounces of sugar and grated lemon rind, and then stir in the semolina and baking powder. Whip the egg whites with a little salt until they are very stiff and then fold them into the mixture. Tip into a greased cake tin and bake in a moderate oven (about 350), for half an hour, until slightly browned.

Make a syrup by boiling together six ounces of sugar and half a pint of water. Pour this syrup over the cake and leave it to cool in the tin it was baked in. Serve the next day with thick cream.

**Elma Kompostosu** WHOLE APPLES STEWED

1 *apple for each person*
1 *cup of water*
4 *ozs sugar*
*Juice and rind of* 1 *lemon*
*A few cloves*

Peel and core the apples and place whole in a deep large pot. Pour the water and lemon juice over them. Put some lemon peel into the water and a few cloves. Sprinkle sugar over all and cover the pot. Simmer until slightly pink and syrupy. Remove to a serving dish and serve with thick cream.

**Helvacı Kabağı Fırında** PUMPKIN TART

*1 pint mashed pumpkin*
*4 ozs moist brown sugar*
*2 eggs*
*A pinch of ginger and cinnamon*
*Juice of 1 lemon*
*Short crust pastry for one 7 ins flan*
*Almonds*

Line the flan dish with the short crust pastry. Cook the pumpkin until soft, drain and mash with the lemon juice, brown sugar, spices and the beaten eggs. Pour into the flan, decorate with some almonds on top and bake in a fairly hot oven (about 375) for half an hour or until the pumpkin is set. Serve with cream.

**İncir Kompostosu** FIGS IN SYRUP

Dried figs are used in this dish.

*1 packet dried figs or 1 lb loose dried figs*
*4 ozs sugar*
*1 pint water*
*Juice of 1 lemon*
*4 ozs walnuts (optional)*

Arrange the dried figs in a pan and pour over them a syrup made with the sugar and water and lemon juice. Simmer very gently until the figs take their original shape again. Serve as they are, or with the broken nuts on top.

**Helvacı Kabağı Kompostosu** PUMPKIN COMPOTE

This recipe comes from Kastamonu on the Black Sea coast and makes an interesting use of pumpkin.

*1 pumpkin of average size*
*4 ozs sugar*
*Juice of 1 lemon*
*2 ozs chopped walnuts and hazel nuts*
*1 tablespoon shredded coconut*

Peel and seed the pumpkin and cut it into cubes. Put these cubes into a pot, add enough water to just cover them and add the sugar. Simmer until soft but not mushy. Tip into a serving bowl and add the lemon juice. Sprinkle the nuts and coconut on top.

### Tel Kadayıf — SHREDDED PUDDING

This dish is made with long threads of vermicelli, but looks and tastes very like shredded wheat, which can be used instead and makes a very good substitute. *Tel kadayıf* is one of the commonest sweets in Turkey and is always a great favourite. It is made in huge round flat dishes and is very sweet and sticky.

8 *shredded wheat (the real tel kadayıf can be obtained from the special shops listed on page 24)*
6 *ozs butter*
6 *ozs broken walnuts*

For the syrup:

6 *ozs sugar*
1 *pint water*
*Juice of* 1 *lemon*

Break up the shredded wheat and lay a layer in a greased baking dish. Sprinkle the nuts over it and put lots of dabs of butter all over it so that it will melt and spread evenly. Repeat another layer of shredded wheat and nuts and dabs of butter. Bake in a moderate oven (370) for about forty minutes until browned on top.

Meanwhile make a syrup with the sugar, water and lemon juice and boil it until quite thick. Then, either allow the *kadayıf* to cool and pour the hot syrup over it, or cool the syrup and pour it over the hot *kadayıf*.

Serve the pudding cold with clotted cream.

### Çilek Kaymaklı — STRAWBERRY CREAM

8 *ozs fresh or frozen strawberries or raspberries*
2 *ozs caster sugar*
1 *egg white*
¼ *pint double cream*

In different bowls, whip the egg white and the cream very stiffly. Add the sugar to the fruit and beat with a wooden spoon until soft and mushy. Then add the cream to the fruit and mix carefully. Finally fold in the white of egg: combine very gently and pile into individual glasses or a bowl. Serve with some extra strawberries or raspberries if available. This amount will be enough for four people.

**Torta** ISTANBUL SWEET

4 *cooking apples*
4 *ozs flour*
3 *ozs sugar*
2 *ozs of walnuts and almonds mixed*
2 *ozs sultanas*
1 *teaspoon baking powder*
1 *teaspoon vanilla essence or* 1 *vanilla pod*
1 *egg*
*Juice of* 1 *lemon*
*A pinch of salt*

Chop up the apples into fairly small pieces and put them in a bowl, then add lemon juice. Mix the dry ingredients (having skinned the nuts) into the apples and finally the beaten egg and vanilla and mix all together. Moisten with a little water if too dry. Put into a greased shallow baking dish and cook in a moderate oven (350) for about twenty minutes. It should be nicely browned on top, but not over-cooked or it will be too dry. Serve hot with cream.

**Çikolatalı Pasta** CHOCOLATE CAKE

Rich cakes are always a favourite and one can sit in a cool cake shop and order a slice of creamy cake which can be eaten with tea or coffee or ice-cream. This is a pleasant interlude to most activities on a hot day. Here is a good rich cake.

8 *ozs butter or margarine*
8 *ozs caster sugar*
4 *eggs*
4 *ozs flour*
4 *ozs cocoa powder*
*A pinch of salt*
*A cream filling*

Beat the butter and sugar together until fluffy, add the eggs and beat well. Now add the flour, cocoa powder and salt; put into a greased cake tin and bake for three-quarters of an hour in a moderate oven (350). Cool and split open and spread a cream filling in the middle and put together again.

### Kurabiye — TURKISH BISCUIT

Ground maize which is the same as polenta or American corn flour is used in this recipe. It has a yellow gritty appearance and is a bit heavy, but tastes good when one becomes used to the difference in texture. It should be very finely ground.

- 4 *ozs sugar*
- 4 *ozs yogurt (or milk)*
- 1 *egg*
- 6 *ozs melted margarine*
- 1 *teaspoon baking powder*
- *(If using milk, add ½ teaspoon of cream of tartar)*
- 8 *ozs maize flour*

Combine all the ingredients except the flour and mix well. Add the flour until you have a stiff dough. Roll into a long thin sausage and slice off rings for baking. (This is easier if, before cutting, the dough is stored in the refrigerator so that it becomes stiffer.)

A variation can be made by mixing half the liquid with four ounces of flour, and half with three ounces of flour and three ounces of cocoa powder. Roll out both into flattish pieces and roll up together so that you have a two-tone effect. Slice off as above.

Bake in a moderate oven (350) for fifteen minutes. To allow for setting, cool before removing from the baking tray.

### Şeftali Kompostosu — PEACH COMPOTE

- 4 *firm peaches*
- 4 *ozs sugar*
- ¼ *pint water*
- *Juice of* 1 *lemon*

Immerse the peaches in some boiling water, and the skin will come off easily. Slice them and put them into a pot with the sugar and water and simmer until they are soft. Add the juice of the lemon and serve.

**Kuru Kayısı Hoşafi** DRIED APRICOT COMPOTE

*1 lb dried apricots*
*3 ozs sugar*
*Juice of 1 lemon*
*1 oz mixed nuts (walnut, almond or hazel)*
*½ pint thick cream*

Soak the dried apricots overnight in enough water to cover them, and then simmer with three ounces of sugar until they are soft and syrupy. Squeeze the juice of the lemon over them and serve with nuts and cream.

**Yassı Kadayıf** TURKISH CRUMPETS

*½ pint cold milk*
*2 eggs*
*2 ozs margarine*
*6 ozs sugar*
*½ pint water*

The nearest thing to *kadayıf* are crumpets, which make a very convenient substitute. Dip the crumpets into the cold milk and then into the beaten eggs and fry them on both sides in some hot margarine.

Make a syrup out of six ounces of sugar and half a pint of water and pour this over the crumpets while they are still hot. They can be eaten either hot or cold.

**Peynir Helvası** CHEESE HELVA FROM MALATYA

There are many varieties of helva and they are made with many different types of flours and nuts; but they usually result in a slab of very stiff paste, which is shaped into blocks and sliced off. They are eaten like sweets and one can buy them by the ounce. There are special shops which make helva and there is a bewildering array of flavours and colours from which to choose. The ones made with nuts and potato flour have the characteristic gritty texture which is crisp and sweet but not cloying.

*½ lb soft white unsalted cheese*
*¼ lb corn flour*
*¼ lb sugar*
*4 ozs butter*
*1 teaspoon vanilla essence or 1 vanilla pod*
*1 cup water*

Melt the butter gently in a frying pan and add all the other ingredients together with one cup of water. Keep turning the mixture over and over and as it dries out it will become a paste. When it feels fairly stiff, tip it out and immediately, before it starts to harden, form it into a slab. Cool it in the refrigerator and then slice off pieces as you want. It should be fairly hard and able to be cut with a knife.

**Dondurma Limonlu** LEMON WATER ICE

*6 lemons*
*6 ozs sugar*
*1 pint water*
*1 egg white*

Peel the lemons and put the rinds into the pint of water and boil together until it has reduced to half a pint. Squeeze the lemons and remove all the pips. Dissolve the sugar in the lemon juice and add to the strained water. Beat the egg white until it is very stiff and mix into the cooled lemon juice. Combine these well together and pour into a freezing tray and put into the freezing compartment of the refrigerator, which should be turned down to its lowest. Leave for twenty minutes; take out and beat thoroughly so that the egg white and lemon juice are no longer separated, and replace in the freezer. Repeat this process until the lemon and egg remain together and it has a thick white appearance.

It is helpful if you can freeze the ice in a deep receptacle as this will make the beating easier. An electric mixer also helps, providing you can keep everything as cold as possible during the beatings.

**Şerbet** FRUIT SHERBET

These sherbets are best made when fresh strawberries or raspberries are in season, but frozen ones can be used. Other fruits that are suitable include cherries, red currants, black currants, apricots and grapes.

Wash and clean the fruit carefully and then weigh it. Put the fruit into a large bowl and add the equivalent weight in sugar. Stir the sugar into the fruit and leave it to dissolve for two days, stirring from time to time.

Strain the liquid through a gauze net and leave to drip until all the liquid is out. A good way of doing this, as one would when making clear jelly, is to turn a kitchen stool upside down and tie the four corners of the gauze to the four legs, and place a bowl underneath it on the upside down seat.

Bottle and seal. These sherbets cannot be stored for too long as they might ferment. They make excellent fizzy drinks with soda water, as well as syrups and milk shakes, and can be poured over ice-cream or puddings.

**Aşure** TRADITIONAL PUDDING

In this very old sweet a little of everything is used. One must start preparing it the day before because of the soaking which is needed. This pudding is much nicer than one might suppose and makes a good dish from odds and ends in the cupboard, when cleaning out the kitchen. This is how it is supposed to have originated, by someone using up everything they could find to make a huge festive pudding.

| | |
|---|---|
| 3 *ozs haricot beans* | 2 *ozs rice* |
| 3 *ozs chick peas* | 3 *ozs sugar* |
| 2 *ozs wheat Buğday* | *Vanilla essence or* 1 *vanilla pod* |

*2 ozs currants*
*2 ozs sultanas*
*Cream*
*Chopped walnuts, pistachios and almonds for topping*

Soak the haricot beans and the chick peas overnight in separate bowls. Soak the rice and wheat together in another bowl.

The next day boil the beans and chick peas in separate pots until they are soft; throw away the water. Boil the rice and wheat together until they are soft and then add the beans and chick peas to them; stir well with a wooden spoon until it becomes like porridge, thick and yet soft. Now add the fruits, sugar and vanilla, and stir them all in until well mixed. Ladle the mixture into small bowls and chill thoroughly. Serve sprinkled with the chopped nuts and cream.

**Dilber Dudağı** LIP-SHAPED FRIED CAKES

*1 lb flour*
*4 ozs butter*
*2 pints water*
*8 ozs sugar*
*3 eggs*
*4 ozs pounded pistachio nuts and almonds*
*1 teaspoon salt*
*Olive oil for deep frying*
*Icing sugar for dredging*

Melt the butter in the water and allow to cool a little; then beat in the flour and sugar gradually until it is well mixed. Add the nuts, salt and eggs and knead into a thick paste. Break off small pieces of dough and flatten with your hands into rounds; fold

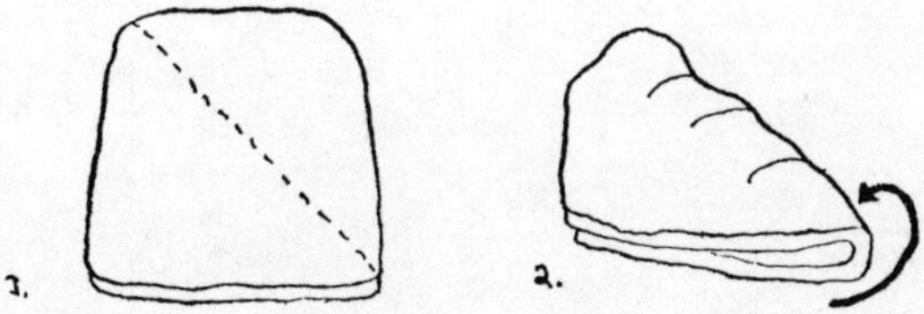

these over to form lips. When they are all ready, fry them in hot deep oil until they are brown, drain them on absorbent paper and dredge them well with icing sugar. Sometimes they are eaten soaked in syrup, but I feel this makes them too rich and sweet.

### Mahallebi — GROUND RICE PUDDING

This sweet is very popular everywhere in Turkey and one often sees rows of little earthenware bowls of it in the refrigerator, together with bowls of yogurt, arranged enticingly in *lokanta* windows.

- 1¼ *pints milk*
- 1 *oz corn flour*
- 1 *oz ground rice*
- 2 *ozs sugar*
- *A few drops of vanilla or a vanilla pod cooked with the milk*

Mix the rice and corn flour together with a little of the cold milk until smooth. Heat the rest of the milk and sugar and when quite hot pour into the rice mixture and stir well. Return to the pan and boil for three minutes or until it thickens, stirring well all the time. It will burn very easily if left. Add the vanilla and pour into small bowls and chill. Ground ginger or cinnamon can be sprinkled on before serving, or cream poured on.

# *Beverages*

**Kahve** TURKISH COFFEE

The difference between the Turkish method of making coffee and the European is that the Turks grind their coffee beans to a very fine powder and then cook it with sugar, producing a thick syrupy drink. Turkish coffee is served in three ways, called *sade*, which is unsweetened, *orta*, which is moderately sweet, and *şekerli*, which is very sweet. One is always asked before the coffee is brewed which of the three one would like.

The coffee should be ground just before it is to be made, and it should be as fine as possible. Put one dessertspoonful of the powder into a small pot with as much sugar as you like, and add one demi-tasse of boiling water. Allow the coffee to boil up and then immediately remove it from the heat. Repeat this process three times, and pour it into the coffee cup. The grains must be given time to subside in the cup before you can drink the coffee and it is helpful to stroke the froth in the cup gently as you wait. Turkish coffee is usually served with a glass of cold water, and it is the custom to take a sip of water after each sip of coffee.

When the coffee is finished quite a lot of black sediment will be left in the bottom of the cup, and a favourite Turkish pastime is to tell fortunes in the grains. The ladies are especially good at this. You are asked to tip your cup upside down on the saucer, so that the grains can run down the sides of the cup forming patterns. After a suitable pause, the cup is scrutinized by the expert and your future is revealed. Some of the predictions are highly amusing, some sinister and ominous!

**Çay** TURKISH TEA

Turkey now grows its own tea, which flourishes around the area of Rize, on the Black Sea coast near Trabzon. It is a very good-quality tea, but still quite expensive. The Turks drink their tea with only sugar, in little glasses about three inches high, with slightly narrowed necks just below the rim. A spoon can thus be balanced across the top with a lump of sugar, which slowly melts into the tea. The Iranians, who share the same tea habits as the Turks, actually drink their tea through the lump of sugar, which is only possible by making loud sucking noises! Most Turks allow the sugar to melt first before drinking. The tea has a light fragrant flavour which is extremely refreshing and one consumes any number of little glasses through the day. Tea is offered during any business transaction and usually helps to seal the bargain. The tea vendors are on every corner and the tea boys, with their brass trays, are seen everywhere swinging along with their little load of glasses.

The tea is made in a teapot, and then left on the top of a special kettle, which has a place to put the pot. It will keep warm there for hours, rather like a samovar, and can be replenished by the hot water in the kettle from time to time.

**Limonlu Çay** LEMON TEA

Lemon tea is considered very good for tummy upsets, as well as colds and Asian flu.

Cut up half a lemon and boil it in a cup of water for ten minutes; just before taking it off the boil add some dry mint or essence of peppermint. Strain the lemon out, and add sugar.

**Çay Karanfil** CLOVE TEA

This tea is thought to be very good for colds.

Make the tea as usual and then add one or two cloves. Cinnamon is sometimes added as well.

**Boza** A MALTED MILLET DRINK

This is a winter drink and is usually sold in the streets at night. One can hear the *boza* boys calling out their ware. It is made from stale bread, which is crumpled into a large pan, covered with water and left to soak until it ferments and becomes sour. It looks like porridge and is very popular with a little cinnamon and milk added.

**Salep** HOT SEMOLINA DRINK

A very thin semolina gruel is made with milk and sugar; about half an ounce of semolina to one pint of milk. It is served in glasses with cinnamon on top and is sold in the streets in the winter. A warming comfort when the winds are blowing down from central Asia.

Although Turkey is extremely hot in the summer, it can be bitterly cold in winter, especially in the eastern districts, near the Caucasus Mountains.

### **Ayran** — YOGURT DRINK

This is a summer drink and is very refreshing and cooling.

- 1 *pint yogurt*
- ½ *pint water*
- *A pinch of salt*

Beat all the ingredients well together and cool. *Ayran* is particularly good with a meal, but is drunk by itself at any time of the day. I remember how very refreshing it seemed on a long hot bus journey from Konya to Ankara, when the *ayran* boys came on the bus at the various stops, selling as much as they could and just jumping off the bus as it drove on!

# *Wines and Spirits*

Turkey, being largely a Moslem country, has never encouraged the production of wine in the past because the Islamic religion forbids the drinking of alcohol. Since 1928, however, when Islam ceased to be the official religion, the state has promoted the manufacturing of wines, beer and liqueurs, as well as permitted the import and sale of foreign spirits.

The excellent grapes which have been grown in southern Turkey since antiquity now form the basis for some very good wines. These wines are being exported under their Turkish names which seems sensible and will avoid confusion when asking for them in Turkey. Among the wines arriving from Turkey, the experts have recommended *Tekirdağ*, a medium white; *Trakya*, which is a dry white, and a full red wine called *Buzbağ*.

There are also some liqueurs which are being exported, among which there is a strong aniseed drink called *Rakı*, which becomes cloudy with the addition of water and is similar to the Greek ouzo. *Raki* is extremely refreshing in a hot climate and goes well with Turkish food. There is also a clear sweet orange liqueur called *Mersin*, named after the orange-growing district of that name in the south, and a *Rose* liqueur, made from fragrant rose petals, which is subtle and mild.

The State Beer Industry produces a good light ale which is reliable and sold throughout the country.

In spite of the apparent emancipation from traditional religious scruples, it is very noticeable that one does not see any drinking in public and there are no pubs or wine shops where people gather to drink alcohol. It is wise to keep in mind, if travelling in Turkey, that drinking is offensive to a strict Moslem, and in out of the way places the religious law is still very much respected.

# Turkish Index

# English Index